The Witch's Christmas Catastrophe

Nocturne Falls
holiday novella

USA TODAY BEST SELLING AUTHOR
KRISTEN PAINTER

THE WITCH'S CHRISTMAS CATASTROPHE:
A Nocturne Falls Novella

Copyright © 2024 Kristen Painter

Welcome to Nocturne Falls, the town that celebrates Halloween 365 days a year. The tourists think it's all a show: the vampires, the werewolves, the witches, the occasional gargoyle flying through the sky. But the supernaturals populating the town know better.

Living in Nocturne Falls means being yourself. Fangs, fur, and all.

Witch Holly Winters is ready for a peaceful, magical Christmas in her family's cozy mountain cabin in Nocturne Falls. She plans to do some knitting and watch all the best holiday movies. But when ancient dark magic begins to stir in the snowy forest, peace and serenity quickly disappear. With danger lurking at every turn, Holly teams up with Demetrius Voss, a brooding and irresistibly handsome vampire neighbor, to unravel the mystery menacing their beloved supernatural town.

As they work together to contain the rising threat, Holly finds herself unexpectedly drawn to Demetrius's quiet strength and unexpected charm. Between Christmas lights, snowball fights, and quiet moments by the fire, sparks begin to fly—proving that even in the midst of chaos, the holiday spirit has a way of bringing people together.

With two quirky cats, a dash of romance, and an epic

battle against ancient forces, Holly and Demetrius must rely on each other to protect the town they love. Will they restore the magic in time for Christmas—and discover that the greatest gift of all is the one they never saw coming?

Demetrius Voss gripped the steering wheel of his black SUV, the knuckles of his leather driving gloves wrinkling as he did. The tires struggled for traction on the ice-slicked mountain road. Snow fell in a thick, blinding curtain, smothering the windshield and rendering his wipers useless against the storm. Even with his vampire senses, seeing more than a few feet ahead was nearly impossible.

"This is ridiculous," he muttered under his breath, his voice barely audible over the roar of the wind. The tires spun again as the SUV fishtailed, narrowly avoiding sliding into the ditch alongside the road. Demetrius cursed, quickly correcting the wheel. The last thing he needed was to slide off the edge of the road and plummet into the thick forest below.

A loud meow from the carrier on the passenger seat made him frown. His cat, Moonshadow, was obviously unhappy, and that bothered him. "I know, Moonie. I'm not thrilled about this either. Hang on. Won't be much longer now."

It couldn't be. He had been driving for hours, trying to make his way up the winding mountain road to his family's estate, Voss Manor. Normally, he could handle treacherous roads without a second thought, but tonight's storm was something else entirely. The roads had already been icy, but then the snow had started unexpectedly earlier that afternoon and now was a full-blown blizzard, howling and furious, as if the mountain itself were trying to force him back.

Maybe it was. Maybe this trip had been a bad idea, but he'd never been one to let that stop him. All he'd wanted was to be alone. To sulk in peace, away from his sisters, who would undoubtedly remind him that his recent breakup was, like the rest of them, a perfect example of the bad choices he made when it came to women.

He couldn't argue that. Esme was painfully beautiful, socially gregarious, but her hidden mean streak had far too often been directed at him. Worse than that, she seemed happiest when stirring up trouble.

What on earth had made him think she was girlfriend material? Beauty was not enough. Not even close to enough.

The Voss manor was perched high on the mountain, the sprawling structure hidden deep within the woods on a road that served it almost exclusively. It had been a few years since he'd been back, but the breakup had drawn him here, his need to be alone and isolated making the Nocturne Falls estate the perfect retreat.

He planned to spend the rest of the winter alone with

Moonshadow, buried in the quiet of the estate's empty halls, far away from the bustling holiday cheer of Nocturne Falls below. Granted, he'd also have the staff that lived on site and maintained the premises. But now, the storm had other ideas.

Demetrius glanced at his cell phone—no signal. Not surprising, considering how far he was into the mountains. Or maybe it was the storm. Whatever the reason, he was irritated by the inconvenience.

He was close to the estate, maybe a few miles at most, but the snow was piling up faster than the SUV could plow through it. The road ahead was disappearing under a thick, icy blanket, and Demetrius could feel the wheels losing their grip again.

Come on, he thought, pressing the gas pedal a little harder. The engine growled in response, but the SUV lurched, slipping sideways as the tires spun helplessly in the snow. The wheels caught for a brief second, then gave way entirely.

With a frustrated growl, Demetrius smacked the steering wheel. The SUV slid to a stop, wedged deep in a snowdrift. "Perfect."

Moonie's meow was plaintive and a little fearful.

"It's okay, baby." Except it wasn't okay. He cut the engine and leaned back in his seat, trying to assess his options.

Walking to the manor would be a nightmare in this storm, especially because he had Moonshadow to look after. Even for him alone, wading through snow that deep would take forever, and the winds were only getting stronger. Demetrius sighed, running a hand through his hair, the storm outside rattling against the windows.

Just then, through the swirling white, he spotted a flicker of light—small but distinct, barely visible through the falling snow. A cabin, he realized. There was someone nearby, and the warm glow of that light meant one thing: shelter.

His eyes narrowed. He knew whose cabin that was. It belonged to the Winters family. They were a family of witches and wizards who'd helped install a magic barrier around both properties as a thank-you to the Vosses for doing some improvements.

Much as he didn't want to be around anyone else, he had no better option. Moonshadow needed warm shelter even more than he did.

With a sigh, Demetrius buttoned up his coat, tugging the collar around his neck. He grabbed his bag from the back, then secured the cover over Moonie's carrier and stepped out into the freezing wind. The cold wind gnawed at his skin, though it barely registered, his vampire blood keeping him from feeling the chill that a human might feel. Still, the snow whipped around him with a viciousness that made it hard to move.

Holding Moonie's carrier tight against his chest, the strap of his bag slung over one shoulder, he trudged through the knee-deep snow, making his way toward the distant light. Each step was a battle against the storm, but the glow grew brighter as he got closer. After what felt like hours but was probably only minutes, Demetrius found himself standing outside a small, cozy cabin nestled in the trees, half-buried in snow. It looked as if it had been plucked from a holiday postcard—warm light spilling out from the windows, smoke curling from the chimney. Even a small, decorated Christmas tree was visible through the windows, the lights twinkling at him.

Without hesitation, Demetrius knocked on the door, shaking snow from his coat as he waited. The sound of footsteps echoed from inside, and after a brief pause, the door creaked open just a crack.

A young, vaguely familiar woman stood there, her brow furrowed in confusion as she peered out at him. She looked about his age—at least, in human years—her wide green eyes blinking in surprise. Dark hair framed her face in loose waves, and she wore a thick sweater that made her look as if she'd been enjoying a quiet evening by the fire before he interrupted.

"Yes?" she asked with a mix of curiosity and concern. "Can I help you?"

Demetrius cleared his throat, realizing how he must look—a stranger, drenched in snow, standing on her doorstep in the middle of a blizzard, clutching a cat carrier to his chest. "My car's stuck in the snow just down the road," he explained. "I was heading up to my family's estate, but the storm caught me. I was wondering if I could take shelter here until it passes."

The woman's concern softened slightly, though she

still looked hesitant. "The storm's getting worse," she said, glancing out into the swirling snow. "You won't make it to the estate tonight."

"No, I won't." Demetrius nodded, acknowledging the truth of her words. "I'll be out of your way as soon as the snow clears."

"Is that a cat?"

"Yes. Moonshadow. She's had all her shots. She won't be any trouble."

"Moonshadow. Of course. You're Demetrius."

"Yes." Realization struck him as she backed away to let him in. "And you're Holly. It's been a while, hasn't it?"

She opened the door wider. "Quite a while. Come in. You'll freeze to death out there. The cat's not a problem as long as she can get along with my Hexi."

Demetrius stepped over the threshold, the warmth of the cabin wrapping around him like a blanket. It was small but inviting, with a fire crackling in the hearth. He glanced around, taking in the simple but cozy decorations—garlands of pine draped over the mantel, a small Christmas tree twinkling in the corner. A brown and black tabby lay on the hearth, taking in the heat with obvious pleasure.

"Thank you, Holly," he said, turning to face her. "I'm indebted to you."

"It's Christmas. And we're neighbors," she replied, offering a polite smile as she closed the door behind him with a wave and twist of her hand, locking the cold outside. "I couldn't let you stay out there. You want coffee or something?"

"I'm fine. Although I'm sure Moonie wouldn't mind getting out of this carrier." Demetrius glanced at the tree and the festive lights, feeling a flicker of something— nostalgia, maybe—at the sight. Christmas had long since lost its magic for him, but here, in this warm, inviting cabin, it felt almost ... comforting.

"Go right ahead and let her out. We'll see how she and Hexi get on." Holly looked him up and down with a mixture of curiosity and amusement. "So, Demetrius, what brings you out here in the middle of a snowstorm?"

"Like I said, I was headed to my family's estate," he said, setting the carrier on the floor and pulling off the cover to set Moonshadow free. He put his bag down as well. "My plan was to spend the rest of the winter there. I didn't expect the storm to get this bad. I really just wanted some peace and quiet."

Holly smiled, though there was a hint of sadness in her eyes. "Well, you came to the right place for quiet. Not much happens up here except snowstorms and the occasional nosy neighbor."

Demetrius chuckled softly, feeling an odd sense of ease in her presence. Despite the unexpected situation, there was something about Holly—something calm and wonderfully normal. He hadn't realized how much he had needed that until now.

Moonshadow sauntered out of the carrier, sniffed the

air a few times, took in her surroundings, then made her way to the couch.

"I hope we're not intruding too much," he said, glancing at Holly. "I don't want to disrupt your Christmas."

Holly's smile softened, her eyes flicking to the tree in the corner. "You're not intruding. Honestly, I wasn't expecting much of a Christmas this year anyway."

Demetrius raised an eyebrow. "Spending it alone?"

She nodded, a wistful look in her eyes. "Yeah. But I guess that's just the way things worked out. My parents went to my brother's place in Oregon."

"You didn't want to go too?"

She opened her mouth, closed it again, then gave him a tight smile. "You sure you don't want coffee?"

"No, thanks." He shouldn't have asked such a personal question. He wasn't sure why he had, really. It wasn't his way.

An uncomfortable silence settled between them, broken only by the crackling fire and the distant howl of the wind. Demetrius shifted, uncertain of what to say. He wasn't used to small talk, especially about holidays and loneliness. Those subjects had long since stopped being part of his world.

"Well," Holly said, clearing her throat and forcing a brighter smile. "Since you're stuck here, you might as well warm up by the fire and make yourself at home. I was going to make some beef vegetable stew. There's plenty if you're hungry."

Demetrius blinked, surprised by the offer. He wasn't used to such casual kindness, especially from someone who was almost a stranger. It had been at least three years since they'd seen each other. She'd been younger then. He didn't remember her being so pretty. "That sounds ... nice."

Holly nodded, heading toward the kitchen. "I'm sure the storm will clear by morning. I hope."

"Same here." Demetrius settled himself on the couch next to Moonshadow. A Christmas movie was playing on the television. His gaze drifted around the room. There was knitting on the chair by the fire, which was giving off a nice warmth. A cup of cocoa sat on the small table nearby.

Obviously, he hadn't expected to end up here the week of Christmas, but maybe this wasn't such a bad place to be after all.

And as the storm raged outside, Demetrius couldn't help but feel that, somehow, this was exactly where he was supposed to be.

HOLLY WAS ABOUT to go into the kitchen when a thought about her new guest popped into her head. She looked at Demetrius. "Are you going to be all right without blood for the night? Because I will not tolerate you snacking on me or my cat."

Demetrius's eyes gleamed with mischief as he

glanced at Hexi. "Tempting, but no, you're both safe," he replied, his voice a cool, deep rumble that somehow managed to be disarmingly attractive while also sounding annoyed.

She glared at him. "Touch my cat and I'll knit silver into your scarf."

Demetrius chuckled—a low and rich sound that caught Holly off guard. "I promise, I wouldn't dream of it. I don't need to feed for a few days anyway."

"Good to know."

He frowned suddenly. "Say, isn't that barrier your family cast around the property supposed to protect against things like this storm?"

"No, sorry. That barrier is there to protect against bad magic, not weather."

He sighed like it was completely useless then.

Good to know he was as handsome and cranky as ever.

His sleek silver cat had taken up residence on Holly's favorite knitted blanket on the couch.

Hexi finally caught sight of her and went under the coffee table. He peeked out at the new addition with uncertainty in his eyes.

To show Hexi that the new cat wasn't his enemy, Holly went to the couch and bent to give the creature a little scratch behind the ears. "Hi, Moonshadow," Holly greeted the cat, who started purring and closed her eyes, pushing her head into Holly's hand. "At least you're not as dramatic as your owner."

Demetrius raised a brow. "I'm not dramatic. And she's a cat. She's inherently dramatic." He looked as though he was fighting the urge to roll his eyes. "Believe me, I would leave if I could."

"I'm sure," Holly muttered under her breath. The Voss lodge, estate, mansion, whatever you wanted to call it, was easily four times the size of this cabin. It resided much farther up the mountain via a private road. Obviously inaccessible by now. The fact that he'd even attempted it seemed to prove his own arrogance. "But for now, you're stuck here with me, Hexi, and Moonshadow. And if you're lucky, I might even knit you a scarf."

Demetrius's lip twitched, almost like he was trying not to smile. Almost. "I think I'll pass. But thanks."

Hexi slinked out from his hiding spot under the coffee table, glaring at Demetrius like the vampire was invading *his* personal domain. Which he kind of was. Moonshadow, meanwhile, had already nestled deeper into the blanket, her eyes half-lidded in contentment. It was as if the blizzard was a mere inconvenience to her luxurious lifestyle.

Cats. Holly nearly snorted at the attitude.

"I better go finish the stew," Holly announced, mostly to fill the awkward silence. "You still want some?"

"Stew sounds good," Demetrius said, his tone surprising her with its sudden warmth. "Even vampires get cold."

Holly arched an eyebrow, her curiosity aroused.

"Really? I thought you were immune to that kind of thing."

Demetrius smirked, running a hand through his damp hair. "Not entirely. Cold blood and all that."

"Well, lucky for you, I know my way around the stove," she said with a grin, heading to the kitchen. She got to work, browning the meat and chopping veggies. As she stirred the pot on the stove, the aroma of garlic, meat, and vegetables filled the small cabin, mixing with the scent of pine and burning wood. It was the kind of comforting smell that made her *almost* forget the blizzard raging outside. The stew simmered gently, releasing bursts of savory aromas and making her mouth water.

Demetrius looked oddly out of place on the couch, like an ancient portrait that had been awkwardly placed in a cozy Christmas card scene. His tall frame, dressed in a black cable sweater and dark jeans, was a stark contrast to the colorful, knitted throw pillows and cheerful holiday decor. But there was something almost peaceful about the way he looked. As if he belonged.

Which he clearly did not.

Even so, Holly found herself glancing at him more than once as she worked, trying to reconcile the stoic vampire with the man currently looking more relaxed than she'd ever seen him.

She distracted herself by making a pan of cornbread. Nothing fancy, it was from a box mix, but she hadn't counted on company, so this would help round out the meal.

When the cornbread and the soup were done, she sliced the cornbread into wedges and set the cast iron pan on a trivet on the table. Then she took heavy crockery bowls from the cabinet. "Stew's ready if you want to come in."

He did, making the kitchen seem a lot smaller suddenly as he took a seat at the table.

"So," Holly said, ladling soup into the bowls. "Why would a broody vampire like you come to a festive town like Nocturne Falls for peace and quiet?"

Demetrius raised an eyebrow, accepting the bowl she handed him. "I live here. And there are no attitude requirements. Thankfully."

"You don't live here year-round, though," Holly said, settling into the seat across from him.

"I don't live anywhere year-round. But I might be here for a while."

That was news. From what she understood, the Vosses had estates in several states and a few countries. "But you've got to admit, you seem more ... Halloween than Christmas."

His expression said her appraisal had slightly amused him. "And you're more Christmas than Halloween. Yet here we are. Maybe we balance each other out."

"Maybe." As Holly brought the cornbread to the table, she rolled her eyes but couldn't help the smile tugging at her lips.

She sat, and they dug into the meal. She took a spoonful of stew, pleased at how good it tasted. The warmth of it spread through her body, and she glanced at him over the rim of her bowl.

"This is good. Thank you for sharing with me." He seemed to be genuinely enjoying the food, so maybe he wasn't just saying it to be nice. In fact, maybe being snowed in with a brooding vampire wasn't the worst way to spend Christmas after all.

As long as he didn't eat her cat.

The storm outside howled like an angry beast, but inside the cabin, it was almost peaceful. Now that dinner was over and cleaned up, which Demetris had offered to help with but Holly had declined, she was back to her knitting. Her fingers worked rhythmically through the yarn, her knitting needles clicking in a steady rhythm that filled the quiet. The fire crackled in the hearth, casting a soft golden glow over the room, and the scent of the home-made stew still lingered in the air.

Demetrius sat across from her, seemingly at ease in the armchair that Hexi usually favored—although the vampire had earned several cold, judgmental glares from the cat since taking his seat. Moonshadow, meanwhile, had remained comfortably on the couch, her shining silver fur quite a contrast with the colorful knitted throws.

Although a new Christmas movie was playing on the television now, Holly found herself distracted from her knitting by watching Demetrius. He was staring into the fire, his angular features softened by the flickering light. For a moment, she allowed herself to study him—his chiseled jaw, the way his dark hair fell in rakish waves over his forehead, and those piercing gray eyes that seemed to glow in the firelight.

Not bad for an undead brooder, she thought with a wry smile.

For a long time, neither of them said a thing. Holly knitted. And Demetrius ... brooded.

"You know, I didn't expect to have a vampire as a houseguest over Christmas," Holly said, breaking the silence. "I figured it'd just be me, Hexi, and my knitting."

"I don't suppose you did." Demetrius turned his gaze toward her, raising an eyebrow. "Just like I didn't expect to be snowed in with a witch who knits cat sweaters."

"Correction," Holly said with a grin, holding up her half-finished creation. "I knit *Hexi* sweaters. I wouldn't feel right calling myself a cat-sweater knitter until I've made one for Moonshadow, too."

Demetrius chuckled softly, surprising Holly. It was a warm, rich sound—unexpectedly human for someone who generally looked like he was pondering the meaning of life eternal and whether it was worth continuing.

"I'd pay to see that," he said, his eyes twinkling with amusement. "Moonie in a sweater. She'd never forgive me. Or you."

Holly laughed, imagining the haughty silver creature wrapped in one of her colorful, fuzzy creations. "True. She'd probably curse you before clawing me to shreds."

Demetrius smirked, his gaze drifting to the fire again. "So, what's with the knitting anyway? I thought witches were more into potions and spells." He wiggled his fingers. "Eye of newt, toe of bat. That sort of thing."

"Toe of bat? Really?" Holly snorted as she pulled another length of yarn through her needles. "I do spells and all that, but knitting is ... different. It's calming. Plus, you'd be surprised at how many enchantments I can work into a piece."

Demetrius raised an eyebrow. "Like what? Can you make a scarf that gives you the ability to fly?"

She grinned mischievously. "Well, I haven't gotten quite that far. But I did knit a scarf that repels bad luck. Gave it to my parents' neighbor last year. He swears he hasn't had a single bad day since."

Demetrius leaned forward slightly, intrigued. "Interesting. So, knitting is your magic specialty?"

"You could say that," Holly said with a nod. "It's practical magic, in a way. Weaving spells into something useful, like a blanket or a pair of mittens. It's how I learned to focus my power. When I'm knitting, everything just ... clicks. No pun intended."

Demetrius went silent for a moment, watching her hands as she worked the needles effortlessly. After a few more seconds, he quietly said, "I get that. Having something to focus on. Keeps the mind from wandering too far."

Holly glanced at him, sensing there was more to his words than he was saying. She knew a little about Demetrius's family—how they'd come to Nocturne Falls years ago to build a family haven. She'd had a few brief interactions with him, seen him in passing, that sort of thing, but he wasn't like the other vampires in town, who were more social and integrated into the quirky community. Demetrius always kept to himself when he was here, keeping a healthy distance from most of Nocturne Falls' residents.

Most of them probably had no idea who he was. She only did because her family's cabin was the last residence before his family's lodge and years ago, his family had asked her family for permission to pave the road, the first half of which was on the Winters property.

The Vosses had offered to include the Winterses' driveway, proposing to do it at no cost to her family. The Vosses had also needed the Winterses' permission to access that brief stretch of the Winters land. Holly's father had granted the necessary rights, creating a friendship between the two families.

As a further thank-you, Holly's mother and grandmother had bespelled what was now known as the Winters-Voss barrier, done to protect both properties from all kinds of magic, although obviously not storms, as the one raging outside proved.

"So you came up here for peace and quiet. Is the rest of your family here?" Holly asked, curiosity getting the best of her. "You don't seem like the 'gathering around the Christmas tree' type."

The corner of his mouth twitched, though there was a distant look in his eyes. "No, I suppose I'm not. And it's just me. My family is in the Alps. I just needed some space."

Holly paused her knitting. There was hurt in his eyes, but he didn't seem to want to talk about it. She understood. "Everyone needs space sometimes."

Demetrius nodded, his eyes fixed once again on the fire. "It's strange. I've lived for centuries, but there's something about the holidays that makes time feel ... different. More important. Like I should be doing something more. Something meaningful." He frowned. "But I never quite know what."

Holly's heart gave a little tug at the vulnerability in his voice. "I get that. Christmas can be overwhelming, even for us magical types. All the pressure to be happy, to be together, to make memories ... Sometimes, it's okay to just take a step back and let yourself feel whatever you need to feel."

Demetrius said nothing, but his gaze flicked to her, and for a moment, the room felt warmer, as if the fire's glow had reached her heart. There was something comforting about the way they were sharing space—two supernatural beings, each dealing with their own baggage, finding an unexpected connection in the middle of a blizzard.

"Do you ever miss it?" Holly asked softly. "The human things, I mean? Christmases before you were, that is, when you were ... alive?"

"I've never been human or technically alive."

"Right. I knew that." She cringed as she realized she

had known that but just forgotten it. Her parents had explained that to her and her brother about the Voss descendants years ago.

Even so, his face darkened for a moment, the trace of sadness in his expression unmistakable. He leaned back in the chair, his hands gripping the armrests, as if he needed to hold on to something. "There are things I miss. The world has changed so much. The traditions, the people, the attitudes ... But every now and then, there's something that reminds me of what things were like. The warmth. The laughter. That sense of ... belonging."

He suddenly shook his head. "Forget I said any of that. It's sappy. And I do not do sentimental."

"It's not sappy. It's honest," Holly shot back, feeling a pang of empathy. She had only lived a fraction of the time he had, but she knew the ache of missing something that had once brought comfort. "You're allowed to feel whatever you're feeling. And you belong here, too, you know. In Nocturne Falls. It might be kind of weird, yeah, but it's as much your home as it is anyone else's. You don't have to spend Christmas on the outskirts, alone."

Demetrius met her gaze, and for a second, his cool, indifferent demeanor cracked, revealing a hint of something deeper. Something just a little bit broken. "Maybe," he said quietly. "I guess I'm still figuring out what home feels like."

Holly smiled softly. "Well, you're welcome here, at least until the snow clears. I mean, Hexi is pretty territorial, but Moonshadow seems fine with it."

As if he'd been listening, Hexi shot Demetrius a withering glare from his spot on the hearth, while Moonshadow, still nestled regally in the blankets on the couch, purred contentedly.

"I'll keep that in mind," Demetrius said, a ghost of a smile tugging at his lips. "I doubt Moonshadow has any interest in giving up her spot anyway. Looks like she's exactly where she wants to be and has no plans to move."

Holly chuckled, setting her knitting down in her lap. "Cats are just like that. They know what they want, and no one can tell them differently. They're like furry little dictators."

Demetrius's eyes twinkled with amusement as he glanced at his cat. "She'd agree with you."

They sat in companionable silence for a while, the sound of the movie, the crackling fire and the soft purring of the cats filling the cabin although not quite drowning out the occasional gust of wind outside. Holly felt an unexpected sense of contentment, knowing that despite the snowstorm, she wasn't alone. There was something comforting about Demetrius's presence—steady, quiet, and surprisingly warm for someone who seemed determined not to lose hold of his hard exterior.

As the evening wore on, the combination of the fire's heat and the soft glow of the lights on the little Christmas tree lulled Holly into a peaceful sense of nostalgia. Not that she'd ever spent the holidays with a vampire before. She glanced at Demetrius, who seemed equally at ease, his usually sharp features relaxed.

"Do you want some hot chocolate?" Holly asked, sitting up straighter. "I make a pretty mean cup." She wanted one, and it wouldn't be polite not to at least ask him.

Demetrius's eyebrow lifted. "Does it involve blood?"

"Okay, gross." Holly laughed. "No. Just cocoa, marshmallows, and a little magic. Trust me, it'll be the best thing you've tasted in centuries." A bold statement to make, but she felt pretty sure she could back it up.

He hesitated, then shrugged. "All right. I'll have a cup. Hard to resist when you sell it like that."

Holly stood and padded into the kitchen, her wool socks muffling her footsteps on the wooden floor. She set to work making two mugs of hot chocolate, getting out a pot and doing it the old-fashioned way. She added milk and the high-quality cocoa she'd ordered online from a Swiss supplier, then stirred in a bit of cinnamon, vanilla, and sugar.

As the brew heated, a sweet aroma began to fill the air. For good measure, she wiggled her fingers over it, spelling it to be delicious. She couldn't help but smile at the absurdity of it all—making hot chocolate for a vampire just days from Christmas in the middle of a blizzard.

If someone had told her this was how she'd be spending the holidays, she would have knitted them a hat just to hide their foolishness.

With the cocoa done and steaming in the mugs, Holly brought them back to the living room and handed one to

Demetrius. He eyed it suspiciously for a moment before taking a cautious sip. His eyes widened slightly, and Holly grinned.

"Good, right?"

Demetrius swallowed, nodding. "I must admit, better than I expected."

"I told you," Holly said with a laugh, taking a sip from her own mug. The rich, sweet taste warmed her from the inside out, and she curled up in her chair, savoring the cocoa and the moment.

They drank in comfortable silence, the raging snowstorm outside no longer feeling so ominous. Inside the cabin, the world was warm and safe, and Holly couldn't help but feel as though something had shifted between her and Demetrius. It wasn't just the snow that had brought them together—it was something deeper, something neither of them had anticipated.

Or maybe she'd watched too many Christmas movies.

As the night stretched on, Holly found herself slouched further into the chair, her eyelids growing heavy. Demetrius, too, seemed more relaxed, his usual guarded expression softened by the warmth of the fire and the quiet of the evening.

In that moment, she realized that maybe—just maybe —Christmas had brought her something she hadn't known she needed. Not just a warm fire, a quiet evening, and an unexpected companion.

But the beginning of something truly magical.

Holly woke the next morning to the sound of soft purring and the weight of something warm and solid nestled against her side. Blinking her eyes open, she found Hexi sprawled lazily next to her, leaning on her hip.

His tail flicked in what was his typical early morning irritation. It didn't matter what time she woke up, it was never early enough for him and his feeding schedule. Hexi liked his breakfast. And to be honest, his lunch and dinner, too.

"Good morning to you, too, you handsome grump," Holly mumbled, rubbing her eyes as the events of the previous night slowly came back to her. The storm, the vampire, the hot chocolate ... and the fact that she had somehow fallen asleep on the couch. She didn't remember moving from the chair. Had Demetrius put her here?

Someone had also covered her with one of the knitted blankets, and Moonshadow was curled at her feet, not seeming to mind the company in the slightest. Even her knitting had been placed back into her yarn bag.

Demetrius, on the other hand, was no longer in his armchair. In fact, he was no longer in sight. Had he gone to sleep in the other bedroom? The space where he had sat was empty, save for a neatly folded blanket draped over the back.

Holly stretched, carefully moving Hexi off of her, and got up. The fire was still going, so Demetrius must have added wood to it. She made her way to the window. The snow had stopped falling, but everything as far as she could see was blanketed in a thick layer of glittering white. The world looked peaceful and serene, as if Nocturne Falls itself had been wrapped in a cozy winter spell.

She yawned, her breath fogging up the window slightly, and turned back to the room. Demetrius's absence worried her for a moment—had he gone out into all of that snow? Vampires weren't exactly known for taking early morning walks, but she wasn't sure what his usual routine was like.

What she did know, although it had briefly slipped her mind, was that Demetrius, just like his siblings, had been *born* a vampire from two vampire parents. Not turned. That made it possible for them to daywalk, unlike their parents, who had both been turned.

With the sun's rays not an issue, maybe he'd made the trek to his family's place to check on things. No doubt that would be on his mind.

Before she could dwell any further on what he might be up to, she heard the soft creak of the kitchen door, and a moment later, Demetrius appeared, carrying a bundle of firewood. He stepped inside, little clumps of snow still stuck to his boots, his angular features made even sharper by the morning light.

"Good morning," he said, his voice low and smooth, as if he had already been awake for hours. Which he probably had been. Vampires didn't need as much sleep as everyone else, did they?

"You're up early," Holly remarked, brows lifting. Despite what she'd just been thinking about, she decided to tease him. "I thought vampires slept until noon."

Demetrius shot her a look as he set the firewood in the log holder by the hearth, then went to hang his coat up. "Contrary to popular belief, I don't sleep all day. Or in a coffin."

"Did you sleep at all?"

"I did. Some. I made coffee, too."

"Thanks. I'll definitely be having some of that." She headed for the kitchen but stopped halfway. "Want some breakfast? I was thinking pancakes and bacon."

"None for me, but thanks."

"Really? You can say no to pancakes and bacon?" With a shrug, she went into the kitchen.

"I can say no to a lot of things." Demetrius followed her into the kitchen, and Holly could feel his aura behind her—quiet but steady and very much present, like a shadow that was more than it seemed.

"Come on," Holly teased, pouring herself a cup of coffee. Once she'd fixed that with creamer and sugar, she opened a cupboard to pull out a bowl and the box of pancake mix. "You've got to eat *something*. How do you get through the day without the magic of carbs and the power of protein?"

Demetrius leaned against the counter like none of this interested him, and yet, he was still there. Watching her. Being part of what she was doing. "I manage. Besides, I thought witches survived on potions, herbal tea, and sage smoke."

Holly laughed, shaking her head as she went back to the fridge for the bacon and an egg for the pancake mix. She measured the mix into the bowl. "Not hardly. I run on sugar, caffeine, and a healthy dose of chocolate. But mostly, this witch needs pancakes like vampires need blood."

The look on Demetrius's face was somewhere between amused and skeptical, but Holly didn't miss the way his eyes softened ever so slightly. There was something about Demetrius—something deeper than his brooding exterior—that intrigued her. He wasn't just some grumpy vampire lurking in the darkness. He had a past, a story, and beneath it all, a heart.

As hard as that was to believe at times.

She cracked an egg into the batter and stirred, feeling his eyes on her, watching her work with a quiet intensity. It was a little unnerving but not entirely unpleasant. The cabin, usually so still and solitary, felt different with him there. Less lonely for sure, but there was an energy she'd never felt before.

She chalked it up to the vibrations of his vampire magic. Like most witches, she was in tune to such things.

That had to be what she was picking up on.

Once the pancakes were sizzling on the griddle and a tray of bacon was in the oven, Holly turned to face him, leaning against the counter just like he was. "So, tell me. Why Nocturne Falls? I mean, it's kind of a strange choice for a vampire who seems to want nothing to do with the whole 'community' thing."

Demetrius's gaze shifted from her to the floor and back again, as if weighing how much to say. "It's quiet in the mountains," he replied after a moment. "For the most part."

Holly raised her eyebrows. "Maybe it's quiet up here, but not in town. This place celebrates Halloween every day. There are tourists everywhere, events every month, and the occasional gargoyle flying overhead. Quiet is not a word I'd use to describe the town."

Demetrius smirked. "Which is why I never go into town if I can help it. Although when I do, no one bats an eye at someone like me. This place thrives on strange and different. The tourists probably think I'm part of the scenery. In fact, I blend right in."

Holly snorted, carefully flipping the pancakes, then dipping her head to check on the bacon through the oven window. Nearly done. "Sure, that's what you do. You blend." She gestured to him with the spatula, taking in his most likely cashmere sweater, expensive jeans, polished boots, and the general vibe of *I'm too cool for this.* "You totally scream 'normal guy.'"

Demetrius pursed his lips, his eyes glinting with

amusement. "Fair enough, but for Nocturne Falls, it works."

Holly had to give him that. The town was a haven for supernaturals that wanted to hide in plain sight. She lifted the cooked pancakes off the griddle and set them on her plate, then got the bacon out and added two slices alongside the pancakes. She turned off the oven and poured two more circles of batter onto the griddle, her mind buzzing with curiosity about the vampire standing in her kitchen. "But seriously, Demetrius. You don't exactly strike me as the type to settle down in a small town. You really think you'll stay here?"

Demetrius hesitated, then shrugged, his expression guarded. "I've lived in a lot of places over the years. Nocturne Falls might as well be one of them. Yes, it's full of strange, magical creatures, but that's part of what I like about it. It feels more welcoming. A little more like home."

Home. The word lingered in the air, more fraught than Holly expected. She sat down at the table, surprised when he joined her. She watched him carefully. She wanted to ask more, to dig deeper, but something told her to tread carefully. Demetrius wasn't the type to spill his entire life story over pancakes. Especially when he wasn't even eating them.

Still, the fact that he had shared even that much with her felt like progress. Maybe there was more to Demetrius Voss than met the eye.

There had to be, right?

As Holly dug into her pancakes, the warm, cakey taste bringing her comfort on the cold, snowy morning, she couldn't help but wonder what it would be like to know Demetrius beyond his razor wit and dry humor. He wasn't like anyone she'd ever met before—both frustrating and intriguing all at the same time.

"Well, for what it's worth," Holly said, finally breaking the silence, "I'm glad you ended up here. At my cabin. Even if it took a blizzard to make you hang out with me."

His mouth nearly formed a smile. "I'm glad I ended up here, too. Maybe the snowstorm wasn't so bad after all."

Later that morning, after the breakfast mess had been cleaned up and the fire was crackling merrily again, Holly decided to take advantage of the clear skies. The snow hadn't started back up again, and the sunlight streaming through the windows made the idea of venturing outside for some fresh air pretty tempting.

"I'm going to check the barrier," she announced, boots already on. She pulled on her coat and wrapped a scarf around her neck before tugging on a hat, both items she'd knitted. "Make sure the Winters family magic is holding up the way it's supposed to."

The barrier was impervious to weather, but that didn't stop her from wanting to be sure it was still in good shape. The storm had been a whopper, and this was Nocturne Falls, a place where stranger things had been known to happen. Stranger things like yetis, for example, but thankfully, their appearance had happened years ago.

Demetrius glanced up from where he sat on the couch reading a thriller he'd plucked from her bookshelves, his long fingers idly stroking Moonshadow's fur. "Want some company?"

Holly blinked, surprised by the offer. She hadn't expected Demetrius to volunteer for a walk in the snow, let alone that he'd want to spend more time in her company. Still, she wasn't about to turn down the opportunity. Maybe he'd open up to her again.

"Sure," she said with a smile. "An extra set of eyes might be useful."

He got bundled up, too, then they stepped outside. The cold air struck Holly's cheeks like a slap, but it was refreshing, especially after the cabin's fire-roasted interior. Their breath made plumes of icy vapor.

The world was silent, save for the occasional creak of branches weighed down by ice and the crunch of their boots in the pristine snow. The cabin looked even cozier from the outside, with smoke curling up from the chimney, a soft layer of white covering the roof, and the windows glowing with warm light. Even her little Christmas tree was partly visible in one window.

Demetrius walked beside her, his long strides making it easy for him to navigate the snowdrifts. His black coat and dark hair stood out against the white backdrop, but there was something rather serene about him as they walked in silence.

After a few minutes, they reached the edge of the property, where the magical barrier that protected the

Winters and Voss properties shimmered faintly in the air, at least to Holly's eyes, although she imagined Demetrius could probably see it too. She pulled off her glove and placed her hand against the invisible wall of magic. It pulsed under her palm, warm and familiar. It was a little like touching a hot water bottle.

"Looks and feels intact," she said, glancing at him. "As it should. Winters family magic is weatherproof. In fact, this barrier is as strong as the day it was placed here."

Demetrius nodded, his eyes scanning the tree line. "Good. I'm glad to hear that. Nice to know your family's magic is that solid, hmm?"

Tugging her glove back on, Holly couldn't help but smile at the compliment, even if it was more directed at her family's magic than her own abilities. Still, she felt a sense of pride. "It is. Does that mean the Winters magic is stronger than you thought?"

Demetrius looked at her, something unreadable in his gaze. "Perhaps. Maybe even stronger than most people realize."

Holly opened her mouth to respond, but before she could, a sudden crackling sound ripped through the air, followed by a distinct ripple in the barrier and the crackle of magic on her skin. Her heart skipped a beat, and she took a step back, her eyes widening in alarm. "Did you see that? Or feel it?"

"Both." Demetrius's expression darkened, and he stepped forward, his hand brushing against the shimmering wall of magic. "Something's interfering with it. Or trying to."

Holly's stomach twisted with unease. The barrier was supposed to be unbreakable—nothing should be able to penetrate it without the Winters family's permission. But whatever that ripple was, it didn't feel right.

She turned to Demetrius, her voice steady but laced with concern. "We need to figure out what's going on. If something can mess with the barrier, it could mean trouble for the whole town. And that could be catastrophic."

Demetrius's eyes met hers, his expression serious. "Agreed. Let's not wait to find out."

As they turned back toward the cabin, Holly couldn't shake the feeling that something far bigger than a snowstorm was headed their way.

Something magical. Something unknown.

And something that could very well turn Christmas into a catastrophe.

The shimmering ripple in the barrier stuck in Holly's mind, bothering her like an itch she couldn't scratch. She and Demetrius had returned to the cabin, but the unsettling sensation of something tampering with the Winters family's magic hung over her. It was as if the pine-scented air in the cabin was suddenly laced with a quiet yet undeniable tension.

Holly paced by the fire, her knitting abandoned on the armchair. She was a problem-solver by nature, but this was no simple tangled yarn situation. The Winters family's protective barrier was built from powerful magic —centuries old, passed down from witch to witch. It wasn't supposed to flicker or bend, and it certainly wasn't supposed to ripple like someone had thrown a rock into a pond.

"Could be a weather-related disturbance," she muttered, half to herself, half to Hexi, who lounged lazily on the hearth rug, uninterested in magical dilemmas. His only response was to close his eyes tighter. Even as she said it, she knew it wasn't possible.

"It wasn't the weather," Demetrius said, his low voice cutting through her thoughts and reinforcing what she already knew. He was standing by the window, watching the horizon like a hawk, his tall frame casting a shadow across the room. "Something or someone is testing the barrier. That much seems clear."

Holly frowned, biting her lip. "But who would want to mess with it? Nocturne Falls is peaceful enough. There haven't been any rogue magical threats in ages." None she knew about anyway.

Demetrius's gaze came toward her, his gray eyes intensely focused. "Peaceful or not, magic attracts attention. Especially old, powerful magic like the kind Alice Bishop has. And the kind your family guards."

Alice Bishop was the witch responsible for the magic that protected the whole town. She was well known to the Winters family, revered, really. Holly couldn't argue that certain types of magic attracted certain types of people. Often those looking to increase their own powers.

The Winters had always been protectors—they prided themselves on being keepers of the balance between magic and the mortal world. But her grandmother was gone, and her parents were thousands of miles away at her brother's.

Her decision not to go with them was really just because she didn't need the constant reminder that he was married and had given them grandkids, whereas Holly had so far only provided them with a grandcat. Something her mother assured her was not the same.

Anyway, with them all away, it felt very much like the responsibility to keep that balance had fallen to Holly. The thing was, she wasn't exactly a battle-hardened witch. She could knit an invisibility cloak faster than you could say *abracadabra*, but if someone was trying to break through her family's magic, that was a whole different ball game.

Holly tugged at the edge of her hand-knitted cardigan, trying to soothe the nervous energy roiling inside her. "If someone's doing something to the barrier, we need to find out why. And fast."

Demetrius crossed the room, his movements as smooth and graceful as ever. "Agreed. But rushing into it won't help. We need to be careful. Whoever or whatever is doing this may not be working alone."

She hadn't thought of that. She sighed and sank into the armchair, reaching for her knitting needles as a way to keep her hands busy. "Great. Another problem to solve. Just what I needed this Christmas."

Demetrius's mouth twitched in what could almost be called a smile—almost. "Christmas is overrated anyway."

"Spoken like a true vampire, and no, it's not." Holly shot him a frustrated glance, twirling the yarn in her fingers. What a humbug. "Don't you ever get into the holiday spirit? You know, wreaths, gingerbread, cozy fireside chats?"

"I think the caretaker put up a wreath," Demetrius said dryly, raising an eyebrow. "It's probably black."

Holly let out a snort of laughter. "Of course it is."

Demetrius leaned against the mantel, arms crossed over his chest as he watched her. The firelight flickered across his face, casting shadows that highlighted his handsome features. For a moment, the air between them felt lighter, as if the ripple in the barrier wasn't lurking in the back of their minds.

But the moment passed quickly, and Holly could feel the weight of the problem settling back over them as thickly as the snow outside. "What's our next move?"

Demetrius studied her for a moment, his gaze thoughtful. "Strengthening the barrier would probably be a good idea. If someone's probing it for weaknesses, the best thing we can do is make sure they don't find any."

Holly nodded, her mind racing with ideas. Strengthening the barrier was possible, but it would take time—and power. She had some spells up her sleeve, but it wouldn't be easy. "I can do it, but I'll have to get supplies from town. A few herbs, crystals, maybe even some iron dust for additional strength. A little salt couldn't hurt either."

Demetrius straightened, his expression unreadable. "I'll go with you."

Once again, she was surprised by the offer. She had expected him to say nothing and let her handle the magical stuff. It wasn't his thing, after all. "Really? You're offering to help me shop for magical supplies?"

He shrugged, his casual demeanor betraying nothing. "You might need help carrying things. And besides, I'm curious to see what the town looks like this time of year. Not to mention, it's a bit of a walk since driving's not an option, and not one you should do alone. Could be slippery."

Holly smiled, feeling an unexpected warmth spread through her. Did he actually care what happened to her? Sounded like it. "Well, who am I to say no to a shopping buddy?"

An hour later, bundled up in scarves, coats, and gloves, Holly and Demetrius made their way down the mountain toward the heart of Nocturne Falls. It was slow going, the main road still unplowed and so thick with snow that Demetrius took on the role of snowplow, going ahead of her to make a path.

The snow crunched beneath their boots, and the air was cold and crisp with the lingering scents of pine and wood smoke. After days of clouds, the sky was a gorgeous clear blue, the kind that seemed to stretch forever, and the town below sparkled like something out of a holiday postcard.

As they approached Main Street, Holly felt the familiar buzz of magic that always thrummed through Nocturne Falls. It was a town unlike any other—a place where supernatural creatures lived openly and every day was Halloween. Except right now, it was also Christmas. The streets were lined with festive lights and garlands, and shops decorated their windows with twinkling lights and magical displays.

"Doesn't look like many people have dared venture out yet," Demetrius commented, scanning the quiet streets. "Except maybe a few who live in town. Can't say that I blame them."

"I think you're right. Still, it's nice to see that the festive spirit remains alive," Holly said, smiling at the sight of a werewolf dressed as Santa passing by with a sack of candy canes that he was handing out to anyone he saw. She took the one he offered her and returned his "Merry Christmas" with one of her own.

She and Demetrius made their way to The Enchanted Apothecary, one of the newest shops in town where witches could find high-quality spell ingredients. The bell above the door jingled as they entered, and the scents of sage, lavender, and something distinctly earthy filled the air. Shelves were lined with jars of herbs and powders, rows of crystals, an array of candles, scrying bowls, ceremonial daggers, and all sorts of magical supplies.

"Hi, Holly. I'm surprised to see you out today." Flavia Heath, the shop's owner and a sister witch, was petite, with bright hazel eyes, a warm smile, and a gorgeous head of beautiful braids. "But you're in luck. I've just stocked up on my herbs and reorganized the crystals."

"You read my mind," Holly said as she approached the counter. "I'm definitely here to shop. Herbs and crystals are on my list, too."

Holly rattled off her list of needs, and Flavia began gathering the supplies. As she did, Demetrius wandered through the shop, his gaze taking in the shelves of magical goods with a look of mild curiosity.

Holly watched him for a moment, wondering what went on behind those cool, calculating eyes. He was hard to read, but there was something about him that intrigued her—something more than just his centuries-old vampire mystique.

"So, what's got you out and about today?" Flavia asked, adding a small pouch of iron dust to Holly's growing stash of items. "I figured you'd be holed up knitting until New Year's. Especially with this weather."

Holly hesitated, not wanting to worry anyone, but Flavia was one of her newest friends and one of the few people she trusted. They'd already had a couple of girls' nights out and shared a lot over coffee several mornings at the Hallowed Bean. "There's been a disturbance in the family barrier," she said quietly. "Nothing major, but it's enough that I'm taking some precautions."

Flavia's eyes widened, and she glanced over at Demetrius before lowering her voice. "The Winters-Voss barrier? Holly, that's serious. What do you think it is?"

"I don't know yet," Holly said, wishing she had an answer. That would make all of this so much easier. "We're trying to figure that out."

Flavia nodded, her expression turning thoughtful. "Well, hopefully you'll have an answer soon. And you stay safe in the meantime." She tipped her head toward Demetrius. "And if he's helping you, I'm sure you'll be fine."

Holly followed Flavia's gaze to Demetrius, who was currently examining a jar of rough moonstone ore as if it held the secrets to the universe. She smiled faintly, feeling a peculiar mix of gratitude and uncertainty. "Yeah. I hope so."

By the time she and Demetrius left the apothecary, the sun had dipped lower in the sky, casting blue shadows across the snow-covered streets and dropping the temperature even further. Demetrius carried the shopping bag of supplies, so Holly wrapped her arms around herself, her mind already working through the spell she'd need to strengthen the barrier.

"So," Demetrius said as they made their way back toward the road that would lead them up the mountain, "what's the plan?"

Holly exhaled, watching her breath curl out into the cold air. "We'll head back to the cabin, and I'll get ready to reinforce the barrier. It's a tricky spell, but with these ingredients, it should hold. At least for now."

Demetrius nodded, his expression thoughtful. "And if it doesn't?"

Holly met his gaze for a second, her heart skipping a beat. She didn't want to think about that. Reinforcing the barrier was their best option, but if something—or someone, like another witch—was determined to break through, there might not be much they could do to stop it.

Worse still, she didn't think she was qualified to rebuild it. Not alone. She dreaded the idea of having to tell her mother what had happened. Her mom would insist on coming to Nocturne Falls as soon as possible and might even cut short the visit to Holly's brother's place for the holidays.

"We'll cross that bridge when we come to it," she said quietly.

"Right." Demetrius's gaze softened as if he understood what she was feeling, and for a moment, the weight of the situation seemed to lift, just a little. "We'll handle it. Whatever happens."

A spark of warmth came to life inside Holly, despite the cold. "Thanks for saying that. It means a lot."

As they made their way back up the mountain, the snow crunching beneath their boots and the quiet stillness of twilight settling around them, Holly couldn't help but feel a little more hopeful.

Because no matter what was coming their way, she wasn't facing it alone.

Not anymore.

Back at the cabin, Holly wasted no time setting up for the spell. The air inside felt cozier than before, the scents of pine and woodsmoke reassuring, but there was a nervous energy humming through her that she couldn't shake.

She had to get this right. She might have a second chance at it but probably not a third.

The fire crackled in the hearth, casting warm waves of light across the walls, while outside, the snow-covered world seemed still and serene, as if nothing could ever disturb its picture-postcard beauty. But Holly knew better.

Demetrius stood by the window like he was watching for something, his tall frame silhouetted against the soft glow of the setting sun. His gaze seemed to be on the horizon, alert as always, his senses attuned to any disturbance.

Moonshadow and Hexi had claimed their usual spots —Hexi was lazily sprawled on the hearth rug, absorbing all the heat he could while eyeing Demetrius warily, whereas Moonshadow had curled up on the blankets again, her silver fur contrasting with the navy knit she was lying on.

"I need to set up a protective circle," Holly said, her

hands full of herbs, candles, and the various other magical items she'd picked up in town. "If you're planning to brood in the corner while I work, make sure you stay outside the boundary."

"I'm not brooding." Demetrius cut his eyes at her. "But I'll try not to interfere with your witchy business."

Holly pursed her lips but couldn't help the small smile that tugged at them. "I'm serious. If you mess up the circle, it'll ruin the spell. We can't afford for that to happen right now."

Demetrius moved away from the window and went to sit on the couch by Moonshadow, putting his feet up on the coffee table and picking up the book he'd been reading. "Don't worry. I'll behave."

"I hope so." Holly nudged his feet off onto the floor, then set the ingredients on the coffee table and started arranging her things on the open floor across from it. She placed the beeswax candles in a wide circle on the hardwood, marking the boundary of the protective field she was about to create.

The scent of lavender and sage filled the air as she carefully sprinkled the herbs and the iron dust between the candles, whispering a few words under her breath to call up the power that she'd been born with.

The energy in the room shifted as she closed the circle. A subtle hum pulsed through the air like the distant vibration of a glass bell. Holly felt the magic gathering around her, prickling her skin, dancing across her fingertips, responding to her intentions.

This was familiar ground for her—she'd been weaving spells since she was a teenager, and protection spells were practically second nature. But this one was different. This was not something simple to be woven into a scarf. The ripple in the barrier was far more serious, and it weighed heavily on her mind.

What really bothered her was that she couldn't shake the feeling that something or someone was waiting, just beyond the edge of her magic. Watching her to see what she'd do. How she'd respond to that ripple.

Almost like this was a test.

"Are you done?" Demetrius asked, his voice low and calm, as if the shift in the room didn't faze him at all. Maybe it hadn't.

"Not yet." Holly knelt in the center of the circle, placing a small crystal in front of her. The crystal shimmered faintly, catching the light of the fire. "I need to focus my energy into this crystal. It'll act as an anchor, holding the spell in place and strengthening it until I can redirect it outside to reinforce the barrier around the cabin."

She'd seen her mother and grandmother cast this spell before, but watching and doing were very different things.

Demetrius nodded, eyeing her with a steady gaze. "And if it works, the barrier will hold against a second intrusion?"

"It should," Holly said, her brow furrowing as she tried to concentrate. "At least long enough for us to figure out what—or who—is trying to break through. Now, stop asking questions. I need to focus."

Demetrius remained quiet, his presence a grounding force, as Holly began to chant softly. The words of the spell rolled off her tongue like a melody, each syllable infused with power. The air around her pulsed with energy, and the candles fluttered, their flames dancing in response to the growing magic.

Power built inside her, like a storm gathering strength. The crystal before her glowed brighter, absorbing the magic she was creating, the surface gleaming with it. She closed her eyes and pushed all her intentions into the spell, weaving the layers of protection as if it were yarn, drawing on nature around her, on the earth beneath her, on the very air filling the cabin.

The crystal had nearly reached saturation, but as the magic peaked, Holly felt a sudden resistance—a sharp tug, like someone yanking on one of the threads she had carefully woven. How could that be? This had nothing to do with the barrier. She hadn't connected to it in any way. Her eyes snapped open, and she gasped, the spell faltering for a split second.

"Holly?" Demetrius started forward, immediately alert, a touch of concern breaking through his usual calm.

Her hand shot up to stop him. "Don't break the circle. I'm fine."

"What was it?"

"I—I felt something," Holly whispered, her heart

racing. She focused on the crystal, focused on keeping the magic contained within it. They couldn't afford for one bit of it to ebb away. "Like ... someone pulling on the magic I was creating."

Demetrius was at the edge of the circle in an instant, his expression tense. "Someone was trying to interfere."

"Maybe. But this isn't connected to the barrier yet. Which means whoever's doing this is after more than just the barrier."

"That's not good."

"No, it's not. But I need to finish this. Give me a moment." Holly swallowed hard, refocusing her energy. She pushed through the resistance, tightening her grip on the magic, weaving it more securely around the crystal, pushing the stone to absorb more. She wouldn't let whoever was out there break her concentration—not now, not when the spell was so close to completion.

The candles fluttered wildly, and the air in the room grew thick with power, but Holly held steady. The crystal's glow intensified, and finally, after what felt like an eternity, the resistance eased. The crystal accepted the last of the magic.

Holly let out a shaky breath, sitting back on her heels. "It's done. I just have to take this outside before there's any more interference." She grabbed up the crystal, stepped over the boundary of the circle, and ran for the barrier, mindless of the snow and cold.

She stopped at the barrier and pushed the crystal into it, hoping nothing would go wrong. With a flash of iridescent light, the crystal and the barrier melded, the power of each becoming one. The crystal disappeared, the spell it held distributed through the barrier. The protective magic was now locked into place. Thankfully.

As quickly as she'd come outside, she went back in, shivering. She went straight to the fire to warm up, holding her hands out. She looked at him. "It worked. The barrier has been reinforced without any issues. No more intrusions, either."

"And you're okay?"

"I'm fine."

Demetrius's gaze remained fixed on her, his eyes narrowed. "But someone was definitely trying to stop you."

Holly nodded, wiping a bead of sweat from her brow despite the cold she'd just felt. "Yeah. That wasn't just a random thing. Someone out there is not only testing the barrier but making an attempt at other magic sources, too. I don't know why or what they're trying to do, but I felt their interference."

For a moment, they stayed silent, the crackling of the fire the only sound in the cabin. Holly sat in her armchair, mind spinning with possibilities. Who could be behind this? What did they want with the Winters family magic? And why now, during the quiet of Christmas?

Demetrius stood, his entire body tense. "If someone's trying to get their hands on any available magic, they'll try again. They'll try until they get what they want."

Holly nodded, her pulse finally settling down. "Maybe. Or maybe their last effort showed them the barrier is too strong. Either way, we need to be ready. The barrier should hold for now, but I don't really know who or what we're up against, so it's hard to say how long it'll last."

Demetrius's gaze darkened, and Holly could see the gears turning in his mind, already strategizing their next move. His protectiveness was subtle, but it was there— like an unspoken promise that whatever threat was looming, they would face it together.

For that, she was grateful. Even if he couldn't do magic the way she could, it was nice to feel that assurance that he would keep her from danger in whatever way he could.

"I'll keep watch," Demetrius said quietly, heading toward the window. "You should rest. You've done enough for today."

"You really think that's necessary?"

"I don't know. But I don't want to take any chances." He shot a quick glance her way, then went back to watching. "I mean it. You should get something to eat and rest."

Holly wanted to protest, to say she didn't need rest, that she could stay up all night if it meant keeping the cabin safe. But the truth was, the spell had drained her. The effort of pushing back against whatever had been interfering had taken more out of her than she'd realized.

"I'll rest, but I'm not hungry. Maybe later," she

relented, standing up and leaving her knitting behind. "But wake me if anything happens."

Demetrius's mouth moved into what might have been a smile, but the expression vanished as quickly as it had appeared. "I will."

She wasn't sure she believed him, but there was no point in arguing. Holly headed to her bedroom, exhaustion settling into her bones. The cabin was quiet and warm, and even without the glow of the fire, she didn't think she'd have any trouble sleeping.

Hexi followed her, curling up at the foot of the bed with an air of nonchalance. But Holly could feel the tension lingering in the air, the uncertainty of what lay beyond the protective barrier.

As she changed into flannel pajamas, climbed into bed, and pulled the blankets around her, she let her mind drift, replaying the day's events. The ripple in the barrier, the strange resistance in the spell, and the presence of Demetrius —always there, always watching, always ready.

It was funny how quickly she had grown used to the presence of the dark, brooding vampire.

HOURS PASSED, and the woods outside the cabin remained still, but Demetrius's keen senses were on high alert. He stayed at the window, watching the snow-covered landscape for any sign of movement, unable to shake the feeling that something or someone was out there.

His mind turned over the possibilities. Who could be bold enough to tamper with Winters family magic? And why now, during the quiet lull of winter, when the world outside was blanketed in snow and silence? When it was, of all things, Christmas?

He didn't have answers, but one thing was clear—this wasn't over. Not when Holly had felt interference while working on the spell.

Whoever was out there would try again. And next time, Demetrius would be ready. The weight of the small blade he kept on him felt like a reassurance.

The fire crackled behind him, spilling light and shadow across the room, but Demetrius's focus never wavered. The darkness of the night pressed in, along with the quiet unease that came with the knowledge that another presence lurked just beyond his reach.

As hard as he focused, he couldn't keep his thoughts from wandering to Holly. Beautiful, sweet, funny Holly. She was really something. Night and day different than Esme, which Demetrius found incredibly refreshing.

He couldn't help but smile when he thought about the way she had fought through the resistance in the spell with such determination. The way her magic had filled the cabin with such bright energy, even in the face of uncertainty. There was something about her—something that had sparked a sense of connection, however unexpected.

Not something he was looking for. Not even in the slightest, but he felt a real admiration for her fortitude and fearlessness. He couldn't imagine Holly whining about the temperature of her coffee not being just right or the strap of her favorite designer handbag being too short.

He couldn't actually imagine Holly *with* a designer handbag. There was no pretention about her. She was who she was. And that was pretty amazing.

She made his protective instinct come to life in a way no other woman, vampire or otherwise, ever had.

Demetrius shook his head, pushing such thoughts aside. Now wasn't the time to get distracted. Or involved. They had a problem to solve, and whoever was behind the attack wouldn't stop until they broke through the barrier or stole all of that magic. He couldn't be sure what the end goal was.

What he was sure of was that for now, the cabin and Holly were safe. The barrier was holding. And Holly, at least, could rest.

Too bad he knew the peace wouldn't last.

As the first light of dawn began to break over the mountains, Holly woke to the soft sound of purring. Hexi was curled around her head on her pillow, his face buried in her hair. She reached up to pet him, his soft fur comforting.

"You make a great hat," she whispered, smiling.

Through the window, she could see the faint glow of sunlight touching the snow outside. She'd slept all night, apparently. Longer than she'd expected to.

She disentangled Hexi from her hair and sat up slowly, stretching out the stiffness in her muscles. The cabin was quiet, and for a moment, Holly allowed herself to believe that maybe, just maybe, everything would be okay.

But deep down, she knew the quiet was temporary. Something was coming—something that threatened not just the cabin but the magic her family had protected for generations.

And with Demetrius by her side, she was ready to face it.

Whatever it took.

She put her robe and slippers on and went out to the

living room, thoughts of Demetrius and coffee on her mind.

She glanced at the empty armchair by the fire where Demetrius had kept watch through the night. He wasn't there, and the fire had burned down to glowing embers. Even so, the cabin was plenty warm.

Her stomach rumbled, ready for breakfast, but her appetite was dampened by the uneasy feeling that had clung to her since the barrier had been tampered with. Whoever had tested the magic would be back, and they would likely be more aggressive next time.

She'd feel better when she had some breakfast and knew where Demetrius was. Didn't take long. Just as he had the previous morning, he came in through the back kitchen door, arms full of firewood, just as she was scrambling eggs and reheating some bacon.

He nodded at her. "Morning. You're up early."

"So are you. Or didn't you sleep?" Holly's voice was still scratchy from sleep. Toast popped up, ready to be buttered. She made her way past him to pour herself a cup of coffee, hoping the caffeine would help shake off the lingering tension from the night before.

"I didn't sleep, and before you tell me I should have, I didn't need to. Vampires don't work that way. I'm fine. Watching the cabin was more important." He stacked the firewood by the fire, hung his coat up, then came back to add a few logs to the fire, which kicked the flames up.

She had no intentions of arguing. "I appreciate that you did that. It's probably why I slept so soundly, knowing you were keeping watch. Breakfast will be ready soon, by the way. Anything happen while I was out?"

Demetrius had gone to the front windows again and didn't look back, just shook his head. "Nothing so far. The barrier's holding as best I can tell, but it almost feels like it's straining. Like it knows it's being watched."

"I felt that too." Holly got plates out and started serving up the food. "Any thoughts on who's behind this yet?"

At last Demetrius turned to face her, his expression troubled in a way she'd never seen. "That's the problem. I don't know. But there *is* a presence out there—something waiting for us to let our guard down."

Holly frowned as she put the plates on the table. She'd gotten that same thing, too, during the spell, that strange tugging, as if something—or someone—was trying to pull her magic away from her. "If someone's watching, they're probably waiting for the right moment to strike again."

Demetrius nodded, his eyes darkening. "I agree. Which is why we need to be ready."

She took a breath, pouring herself a second cup of coffee. She held it in both hands. The warmth spread through her, chasing away the cold that seemed to have suddenly settled in her bones. "I don't suppose you have any experience with magical barriers, do you?"

"Not personally," he said, coming back into the kitchen, "but I've seen enough to know that whoever's messing with this one is no amateur. They have some sense of what they're doing."

Holly sipped her coffee, the rich, bitter taste erasing the last bit of sleepiness. She took a seat at the table. "Great. So we're dealing with someone who's both powerful and smart. Perfect combination for the holidays."

His mouth quirked into a faint, almost imperceptible smile as he joined her. "Not exactly the Christmas spirit, is it?"

She shook her head, grinning despite the weight of the situation. "No, not exactly. But hey, at least I've got you to help with the supernatural defense strategy."

"Lucky you," he said dryly, though there was a glint of amusement in his eyes.

They ate without a lot of conversation, both of them seemingly intent on getting the meal done.

She ate her last bite of bacon, then took her plate to the sink to deal with later. Curious suddenly, she went into the living room, to the coffee table, where she'd left the crystals she hadn't used in her spell the night before.

She picked one up. It shimmered faintly, its surface warm to the touch, but the energy inherent to it had grown thinner. Almost as if all magic were being affected. "I can reinforce the barrier again later, but I can't keep doing that forever. We need to figure out who's behind this."

Demetrius nodded, moving to stand beside her, a cup of coffee in his hands, too, now. "We can start by asking around in town. Someone must've noticed something unusual. And if not ... we'll just have to dig deeper."

Holly bit her lip, thinking. Nocturne Falls was a small town, and news—especially strange, magical news—traveled fast among the locals. If someone had been tampering with the Winters family magic, there was a good chance someone knew something.

"Right," Holly said, nodding to herself. "We'll go back to Flavia. If anyone knows about magical disturbances, it's her."

Demetrius glanced at her, his gray eyes gleaming with quiet resolve and maybe a little resignation. "I'll go with you."

Despite his past help, Holly was still surprised that he'd offer to do this. "You're willing to help with asking around? You know that involves people, right? Talking to them. Being nice to them. It's a lot of interaction."

He gave her a look. "I can talk to people."

"Without scaring them off?" She did her best not to smile, but she was enjoying this.

"Yes." He frowned, then shrugged, his expression turning as stoic as ever. "I'm already involved, aren't I? And I'm not letting you face this alone."

Warmth blossomed in Holly's chest at his words, and she let her smile come through. "Thanks, Demetrius."

They bundled up again. The walk into town was brisk, the air biting at them as they trudged through the snow. The crunch of it underfoot created a sort of rhythm. At least this time they could use the path they'd carved out on the last walk.

Demetrius stayed close beside her, silent but alert, his gaze scanning the horizon as if expecting trouble to emerge from the forest at any moment.

She really hoped that wasn't going to happen.

The town of Nocturne Falls still looked like a winter wonderland, with snow blanketing the rooftops and icicles hanging from the eaves. The streets were lined with festive lights and garlands of pine and holly. A happy snowman had appeared near the gargoyle fountain in the center of town, no doubt thanks to the talents of some local children.

But the big thing was the main roads were now plowed. It was a good sign that the road up the mountain would be too, soon. Even though it was essentially a private road, she knew Demetrius's family had a contract with the town to take care of such things like plowing and tree removal, should that become necessary.

As they approached The Enchanted Apothecary, Holly felt a surge of hope. Flavia always had her ear to the ground when it came to magical occurrences, and if anyone knew what was going on, it would be her. Just last month, she'd become the Nocturne Falls coven's membership liaison, further extending her personal network.

The woman was connected.

The bell above the shop door jingled as they entered, and the familiar scent of sage and lavender greeted them. Flavia was organizing shelves of potions and herbs, her braids tied back with festive red and green ribbons.

"Holly, Demetrius," she greeted them, glancing between them with a curious smile. "Back again so soon?"

Holly didn't waste time with small talk. "We are because we need your help, Flavia. Now someone is not only tampering with the Winters-Voss family barrier, but my own magic has been affected. And we still don't have any idea who it is. Have you heard anything? Seen anything weird going on around town? Had anyone in shopping for questionable items?"

Flavia's brow furrowed, and she set down the jar of bay laurel she'd been holding. "Now you're having issues? This is getting serious." She paused, her expression turning thoughtful. "I haven't heard anything specific, but there have been some odd disturbances. People have mentioned strange flashes of light near the edge of the forest, and there was talk on the coven loop that several people felt a weird energy shift in the air a few nights ago."

Holly exchanged a glance with Demetrius, her stomach dropping at the news. "That sounds like it could be connected."

Flavia nodded slowly. "It totally does. But whoever's behind it is keeping a low profile. With good reason, obviously. I wonder what they're up to?"

"No idea." Demetrius's voice was low but firm. "But

we need to find out who's responsible before they make another move."

Flavia pursed her lips, her eyes narrowing in thought. "There's a few new witches who've moved to town recently, but there's one who comes to mind right away. She's a reclusive one. Name's Morgana, although that sounds made-up to me. She keeps to herself, but she's been in here asking about ancient magic—family magic, specifically. If anyone's meddling with your family's barrier, she'd be worth looking into."

Holly frowned, the name unfamiliar. "Morgana? I haven't heard of her."

"She stays out of sight," Flavia said, lowering her voice. "Lives in a bungalow on the outskirts of town, near the woods that surround the lake. She's powerful, from what I've heard. Not the friendly type either. I went to welcome her to town and invite her to the next coven meeting, even took a jar of Mattie Sharpe's honey." Flavia cocked one hip out as she crossed her arms. "Witch wouldn't even open the door. I don't think she had a clue I was the one she'd dissed when she came in here looking for information."

Demetrius straightened, a keen look in his eyes. "Sounds like we should pay her a visit."

Holly nodded, her mind already churning through the possibilities. Whoever Morgana was, she seemed like the best lead they had. If she was interested in ancient family magic, there was a good chance she knew about the Winters family's barrier.

"Thanks, Flavia," Holly said, giving her a grateful smile.

Flavia waved a hand. "You bet, but be careful, Holly. Like I told you, Morgana's not the type to welcome visitors." Her gaze shifted to Demetrius. "Not sure what she'll do if she sees a vampire on her porch."

Holly gave a small, determined nod. "We'll be careful. Can you write down her address?"

"Sure." Flavia scribbled it on a scrap of paper and handed it over.

As Holly and Demetrius stepped out of the shop and back into the cold, crisp air, she turned to him, her resolve firming up. "Looks like we've got a lead."

Demetrius nodded, looking less convinced. "Let's hope it's the right one." He glanced toward the direction of the lake. "It's too far to walk. We'll have to take my SUV, but once we get off the mountain, we should be okay on the main road now that it's plowed."

"All right."

They walked back to her cabin, then Demetrius took his time pushing the vehicle out of the snow and into her driveway so he could back out and turn around. When he was satisfied he could handle the drive, he came back inside and got Holly.

He drove cautiously, taking things slowly as they made their way toward the plowed roads. Once there, he picked up speed a little as they headed for the outskirts of Nocturne Falls, past the beautiful frozen lake that held half a dozen ice skaters today, out to where the trees were thick and the snow lay undisturbed by human footsteps. The air was colder here, as if the woods were holding their breath. Holly couldn't shake the feeling that they were walking into something dangerous, but there was no turning back now.

It was probably nothing. She was just on edge from everything that had been going on. Morgana was a sister witch. She had no reason to do Holly any harm.

At least that's what Holly kept telling herself.

Demetrius stayed by her side, his presence both reassuring and a reminder of the stakes. Whoever Morgana was, she might hold the key to solving the mystery of the barrier. But she might also be the one responsible for the attack.

In that case, Holly had no idea what to expect.

He parked, and as they approached a small, single-story bungalow nestled at the edge of the forest, Holly felt a chill that had nothing to do with the weather. The air around the cottage was thick with magic—dark, aged magic that made the hairs on the back of her neck stand on end.

Demetrius's eyes narrowed, and he glanced at Holly. "You feel that?"

"I was just about to ask you the same thing." Holly nodded, her pulse quickening. "This is definitely the place."

They stepped closer, and as they reached the front of the bungalow, the door creaked open slowly, as if inviting them inside.

"Well," Holly muttered, her muscles tight with stress, "that doesn't scream 'danger' at all."

Demetrius's hand moved toward the door, his eyes scanning the shadows inside. "Stay close."

She didn't need to be told twice.

And with that, they stepped into the cottage. The door closed behind them with a soft click, making Holly tense up even further.

The air inside was redolent with the scent of earth and incense, but beneath it, Holly could sense something darker—a simmering magic that sizzled against her skin. The room was sparsely furnished and dimly lit, with candles casting flickering shadows across the walls.

"Morgana?" Holly called out, her voice a little unsteady.

A soft, chilling voice floated out of the darkness. "I've been expecting you."

Holly's breath caught in her throat as a figure stepped into the light, her silhouette tall and slender, her eyes gleaming with a knowing expression.

"Well, this just got interesting," Holly muttered under her breath.

Demetrius's posture changed, as if he was readying himself for any possibility. Holly appreciated his preparedness.

The witch known as Morgana regarded them with a curious, calculating gaze, leading Holly to believe they were in for much more than they had bargained for.

Demetrius tensed, wary as he could be, as the tall figure of Morgana stepped out of the shadows, her eyes gleaming with an unsettling mix of curiosity and power. Her face was lined by time and age, but it was hard to tell just how old she was.

The air in the cottage felt thick, almost suffocating, as if it were charged with a magic that was as ancient as the earth it was built on.

Holly had to be feeling it too. He could hear her heart pounding, but her exterior looked as cool as could be. For reasons he couldn't name, that made him proud of her.

Morgana's presence was striking—her long, deep purple hair flowed down her back like a mystical river, and her pale, wrinkled features seemed to almost glow in the dim candlelight. Her eyes, a shade of blue-violet that Demetrius had never seen before, flicked between him and Holly. Undoubtedly sizing them up.

"I knew you'd come," Morgana said in a voice that was calm but edged with something dangerous. "I've been feeling the disturbance in the Winters family barrier, so I knew you had to be feeling it too."

Holly clenched her fists at her sides, as if trying to

keep her nerves in check. "What do you know about the barrier?"

Morgana smiled faintly, a gesture that didn't reach her eyes. "Just that the Winters family magic is one of the oldest forms of defense magic. I've been studying it and Alice Bishop's magic, older still, that's protected this town for years."

Demetrius took a small step forward, trying to make a point of the fact that Holly was not alone. "And what do you want with it?"

Morgana's gaze shifted to him, but her expression remained unreadable. "You misunderstand, vampire. I'm not trying to harm or steal the barrier's magic. Not in any way."

Holly frowned. "Then what are you doing? Someone's been tampering with the barrier, trying to break through."

Morgana's eyes glinted with a dark amusement. "Not break through. Strengthen."

Holly blinked as if completely taken aback. "Strengthen? Why would you want to—"

"Because there's something coming," Morgana interrupted, her voice low and steady. "Something powerful. And the current barrier won't be enough to stop it."

"How do you know that," Holly asked.

"I just do," Morgana insisted.

Holly's expression said she didn't believe that for a second, but Demetrius could sense the uncertainty in

her. He glanced at her, hoping she could read the silent
question in his eyes.

Holly's glance seemed to confirm she did. She turned
back to Morgana. "Okay, so you know the barrier's not
strong enough. But what do you mean something's
coming? And why didn't you just tell me instead of interfering with the barrier?"

Morgana's smile faded, and she took a cautious step
closer. "Because I wasn't sure you'd listen. Most witches
wouldn't. They'd assume I was the threat and try to push
me away. Didn't you perceive me as a threat when you
saw me?"

Holly narrowed her eyes. "Yes, but with good reason."

Demetrius chimed in. "You should have tried to talk
to Holly regardless. Instead, you decided to do whatever
you wanted with the barrier. That's not exactly a way to
win people over."

Morgana sighed softly, as if disappointed. "I didn't
interfere with your magic. I was trying to reinforce it. The
ripple you felt was me testing its strength—and its weak-
ness. I needed to know its limits."

Holly seemed to be experiencing a surge of frustration, but somehow, she stayed calm. "And why should I
believe you?"

Morgana's blue-violet eyes flashed with an urgent
intensity. "Because I know the kind of magic that's
heading your way. You'll need more than just your family's barrier to stop it."

Demetrius spoke up. "What kind of magic?"

Morgana's gaze moved back to him, and for a moment, something almost like respect passed between them. "Ancient. Dark. The kind of magic that twists and corrupts everything it touches. It's been building, slowly gathering strength in the woods outside of town."

Demetrius felt the seriousness of Morgana's words settle over him like a heavy weight. Dark magic. Ancient magic. Was this something Holly could handle alone? He wasn't sure. And he certainly wasn't equipped to help.

Holly glanced at him before looking at Morgana again.

He would have given anything to offer her a modicum of hope, but magic of this kind was outside of his knowledge.

"And how do we stop it?" Holly asked, her voice steady despite the anxiety she had to be feeling.

Morgana lifted her chin, her gaze thoughtful as she answered. "We can't stop it. But we can contain it."

"Contain it?" Demetrius couldn't keep the skepticism from his voice. If what Morgana said was true, containing this ancient dark magic sounded like trying to hold back a tidal wave with a paper umbrella.

"Yes." Morgana nodded. "We'll need to combine our magic—yours, mine, and possibly others. The barrier needs to be reinforced, and additional wards need to be put in place around the perimeter of the forest. If we can isolate the source of the magic before it reaches full strength, we have a chance."

Demetrius shook his head. "I don't have magic."

Morgana snorted. "You were born a vampire, which gave you the ability to daywalk, and you don't think you have magic? Just because you can't cast a spell doesn't mean you can't be useful."

Even so, Demetrius's mind was full of questions. There was still so much they didn't know about this witch, and despite Morgana's calm demeanor, he couldn't shake the feeling that there was more to the story than she was letting on.

"What's in it for you?" Holly asked, her voice laced with suspicion, making Demetrius think she was having the same doubts he was. "You show up out of nowhere, you know more about my family's magic than you should, and now you're offering to help. Why?"

Morgana's eyes darkened, her voice turning cold. "Because I've seen what this kind of magic can do. It consumes everything in its path. I've dealt with it before, and I don't intend to let it take root here. I hope to make Nocturne Falls my home. To do that, I must protect it."

Demetrius looked at Holly again. There were questions in her eyes. She was clearly weighing the risk, just as he was. Morgana's offer sounded genuine, but they both knew how easily things could go wrong when dealing with dark magic.

Holly took a deep breath and locked eyes with Demetrius, brows raising slightly.

He got it. She didn't fully trust Morgana, but if the witch was telling the truth, then they didn't have much choice. They couldn't afford to let ancient dark magic slip through their fingers and into the town.

He gave her a short nod to let her know he agreed with everything she was thinking. This was her decision to make. It was her family's barrier. Their magic. He'd support whatever she wanted to do.

"All right," Holly said finally, meeting Morgana's gaze. "We'll work together. But if you're hiding anything, or if this goes sideways, you'll answer to me. I don't care how old or how powerful you are."

Morgana's mouth curved into a small, humorless smile. "Agreed."

Demetrius touched Holly's hand to get her attention. "We'll need to act quickly. If the magic is growing, we don't have much time."

Holly nodded. "No, we don't. This wasn't what I thought I'd be doing when I settled in for a quiet holiday, but there's no turning back."

"Same here." Something dark and dangerous was on its way, and they were the only ones standing between it and the town.

Morgana glanced around the room, her eyes settling on the lit candles and the dark shadows that clung to the corners. "I'll need to gather a few things from my bungalow. I'm sure you'll want to get supplies of your own. Meet me at the barrier near your cabin in an hour."

Holly gave a quick nod, as if her thoughts were already working on the next steps. "We'll be ready."

Morgana slipped back into the shadows of the bungalow, her presence vanishing as quietly as it had appeared.

Demetrius grabbed Holly's hand and pulled her
outside, making tracks toward the SUV. He did his best to
keep his expression calm, but inside, he was anything
but.

Back in the vehicle, its doors closed, Holly finally
spoke. "Well," she said with a shaky breath, "that was ...
unexpected."

Demetrius started the engine and put his hands on
the wheel. "Do you trust her?"

Holly hesitated. "No. Maybe. I don't know. But if she's
telling the truth, we don't have much of a choice."

Demetrius nodded. "I know. All we can do is keep an
eye on her. If she's hiding something, I suppose we'll
know soon enough." Hopefully before it was too late.

"Thanks again for coming with me," Holly said.
"Having you by my side makes me feel less alone. More
like I can do this. But don't let that go to your head."

He smiled as he backed the car onto the road. "I'll try
not to." But it made him feel good. He couldn't recall
Esme ever giving him a compliment like that.

As they made their way back toward the cabin, the
SUV's heat kicking on to take away the chill they'd
brought with them from Morgana's, Demetrius knew that
whatever happened next, they would face it side by side.
He would do whatever was necessary to protect Holly.

He just hoped they were ready for whatever was
coming.

As they drove back toward the cabin, the sun was beginning to set. The trees sent shadows across the road as the light changed, turning the world into a mixture of blue and silver. Holly pulled her scarf tighter around her neck, her mind working through everything Morgana had said.

Ancient dark magic, building in the woods outside of Nocturne Falls. That wasn't exactly the holiday surprise Holly had been expecting.

"Do you really think she's telling the truth?" Holly asked, glancing at Demetrius as he kept his eyes on the road.

Demetrius's eyes scanned the horizon. "I don't know. But if Morgana is right, and something powerful is brewing, we can't afford to ignore it."

"No, of course not." Holly sighed, stretched her legs out in front of her. Demetrius's SUV had a lot more room than her car. "I just hate feeling like I'm being dragged into something I don't fully understand. And Morgana— she's hiding something. I can feel it."

Demetrius nodded, his jaw tight. "I got that feeling too. But that doesn't mean she's lying about the threat. Witches like Morgana don't act unless they have a reason, right? Whether or not we trust her, we'll need to be cautious."

"Yeah." Holly held her hands up to the heater vent to warm her fingers. It was more than just the cold that had her on edge—there was something about Morgana that unsettled her. Maybe it was the witch's calm demeanor, her cryptic warnings, or the way her eyes seemed to gleam with secrets. Or maybe it was the way Holly couldn't shake the feeling that Morgana knew more about her family's magic than she was letting on.

"You're awfully quiet," Holly said, casting a sideways glance at Demetrius. "What's going on in that brooding head of yours?"

Demetrius's mouth hitched up on one side, just a fraction, but enough that Holly felt a flicker of warmth at the sight. He wasn't much of a smiler, but every now and then, she caught a glimpse of something softer beneath his cold exterior.

"I was thinking about what Morgana said," Demetrius replied, his voice low. "About the dark magic. If it's ancient, it could be tied to something older than this town."

Holly's brow furrowed. "Like what?"

Demetrius stopped talking for a moment, his gaze remaining on the road ahead as he considered his words. After a few seconds, he said, "Nocturne Falls isn't just a place where supernatural beings live. There's a reason creatures like me, witches, werewolves, and others have been drawn here for so long. The magic that protects this town is older than any of us. It could be connected to whatever is out there in the woods."

"You can't mean Alice Bishop?" Holly's heart skipped a beat. She'd always known Nocturne Falls had its quirks —it was a town that celebrated Halloween three hundred and sixty-five days a year, after all. But she hadn't considered the possibility that something deeper, something more ancient, was woven into the town's fabric. And that it might have come from Alice Bishop.

"I don't know. She's a pretty mysterious figure."

"I agree with that, but Elenora Ellingham wouldn't have anything to do with a woman that could cause her family harm. Or ruin all the hard work the Ellinghams have put into this place. You're a vampire just like they are. You have to know how they'd think."

He seemed to consider that, giving a quick nod. "You're right. But if it's not Alice, then what or who is it? The way Morgana was talking, it's magic that's been here a while."

"So you think whatever dark magic is out there could be connected to Nocturne Falls itself?" Holly asked.

Demetrius nodded. "I'm just saying it's possible. And if that's the case, reinforcing the barrier won't be enough. We'll need to understand what we're dealing with before it grows too strong to contain."

A shiver ran down Holly's spine, and it had nothing to do with the cold. She had always thought of magic as something she could control, something tangible that she could bend to her will. But now, the idea of ancient magic

—older, darker magic—made her feel like she was standing at the edge of a precipice, unsure of what lay below. And very worried she was about to fall.

As they reached the cabin, Holly sent a tendril of magic out to stoke the fire. A moment later, she noticed a glow spilling out through the windows, casting a golden light onto the snow. The sight made her feel better, as though her magic really might be enough. As if the walls of the cabin could keep whatever was lurking in the woods at bay.

Demetrius parked and followed her inside, and the door creaked shut behind them, sealing out the cold. Holly pulled off her gloves. "We should eat before we meet Morgana. I can heat up the leftover stew."

"Sounds good. While you do that, I'll bring more wood in and build up the fire."

"Great." Hexi trotted over to greet her, his yellow eyes full of love as he weaved between Holly's legs.

"Yeah, yeah, I missed you too," Holly murmured, bending down to scratch Hexi behind the ears. The cat purred contentedly before sauntering off to his favorite spot by the fire, where Moonshadow was already curled up, her silver fur gleaming in the firelight.

Apparently, she and Hexi had become friends.

Holly straightened, her eyes drifting to Demetrius as he shed his coat and hung it by the door. Despite the tension of the day, his presence was a comfort. The way he always stayed calm, the way he always seemed so in control, the way nothing seemed to ruffle him, even when everything around them was getting more uncertain by the second.

"You think Morgana's really going to show up?" Holly asked, moving toward the fire to warm her hands for a few seconds.

Demetrius nodded. "She'll come. She's too invested not to. But if she doesn't ... I guess we'll know we've been played."

Holly sighed as she went into the kitchen to get the stew ready. She heated it up on the stove and, as soon as it was hot, filled two bowls. They sat at the table to eat, their conversation returning to the matter at hand.

Holly swallowed the spoonful she'd just taken. "I wish I knew more about this ancient magic. My family's magic has always been protective, but I've never dealt with anything like this before. Black magic, gray magic, anything like that, we've never messed with it. Most witches I know won't go near the stuff."

Demetrius, who sat across from her, downing the stew as though his appetite had suddenly kicked in, gestured at her with his spoon. "You're stronger than you think, Holly."

Holly tried to find the right words to tell him how much she appreciated his support. It really did mean a lot. But all she could come up with was, "I hope you're right."

They finished the stew, and he helped her clean up, which didn't take long. "Need any more help?" he asked. "Like with the magical stuff?"

She opened her mouth to respond, but before she could say anything, there was a sharp knock at the door.

Both she and Demetrius tensed. She shot him a look, and he nodded silently, moving to stand by the door, ready for anything. Holly followed him, pulse thumping. She reached for the door handle, wondering who it could be.

When she opened the door, Morgana stood on the other side, her dark eyes gleaming in the fading light.

"You're early," Holly said. It hadn't even been forty-five minutes yet. The faint aroma of stew still wafted through the air.

"There's no point in waiting any longer, so I hope you're ready," Morgana said, her voice clipped. She stepped inside without waiting for an invitation, her presence as commanding as ever. "We don't have much time."

Holly exchanged a glance with Demetrius before turning to face Morgana. "I thought we had more time, but we can be ready in a few minutes. I just need to gather a few things. But I want to know exactly what we're up against. Tell me everything you know. Hold nothing back."

Morgana's lips pressed into a thin line as she glanced at the two of them. "As I told you, the magic I've been sensing is old—older than this town, older than any of us. I believe it's been dormant for centuries, but something has awakened it. I don't know what triggered it, but if we don't contain it soon, it will spread. And when it does, there won't be anything left to stop it."

Holly's stomach twisted at the magnitude of Morgana's words, but at least it didn't sound like Alice was behind this. "So what do we need to do?"

Morgana stepped closer, her eyes locking onto Holly's. "You and I will need to combine our magic to strengthen the barrier. Doing that might be enough to keep these dark forces at bay. Demetrius will need to keep watch for any signs of the dark magic breaching the perimeter. With his permission, we can also boost our own magic through the use of his."

He frowned. "How does that work?"

"We simply treat you like a magical battery. You'll feel us reaching for you. As long as you don't fight our attempts, your inherent magic will give our work support."

Holly could tell by the tightening of Demetrius's jaw that he wasn't so sure about that. After a second, he nodded. "Fine. But what if none of this works? What if the barrier isn't enough?"

Morgana's gaze hardened. "Then we'll have no other option than to fight whatever or whoever is doing this."

Holly swallowed. She wasn't prepared for this—she hadn't trained for ancient dark magic battles. Or any kind of magical battle, really. But she didn't have a choice. If Morgana was right, the town was in danger, and it was up to them to stop whatever was coming.

"We'll do everything we can," Holly said, her voice steady despite the fear gnawing at her insides.

"Good. We're close enough to the barrier here. We

can begin now. Follow my lead." Without another word, Morgana moved to the center of the room, her hands already beginning to trace intricate patterns in the air.

Holly had seen her mother and grandmother do this kind of spell-casting. She mimicked the pattern, her fingers moving instinctively, the familiar tingle of magic buzzing at her fingertips.

Demetrius took up his usual spot by the window, his posture tense as he kept watch over the snow-covered forest. Outside, the wind had started again, swirling the snow into small flurries that danced in the fading light.

As Holly focused on the spell, magic gathered in the air around her, making it heavy with energy. The candles flickered wildly, their flames growing taller, brighter. She closed her eyes, letting the power flow through her, feeling it twist and coil with Morgana's magic, weaving together like threads in a tapestry.

She felt Demetrius's presence, too. It gave her strength, more than she'd ever felt before.

The magic pulsed, filling the room with a low hum, and for a moment, Holly felt a surge of hope. They were doing it—they were reinforcing the barrier in a brand-new way.

But then, just as quickly as it had begun, something shifted.

The air grew colder suddenly, as if a deep, unnatural chill had crept into the room. Holly's eyes snapped open, and she saw it through the windows—the murky, swirling energy at the edge of the property, pressing against the barrier like a dark spirit trying to break free.

Demetrius tensed as he watched the dark magic pulse against the barrier. The look in his eyes was unsettling.

"Morgana," Holly said, her voice sticking in her throat, "something's happening."

Morgana's gaze narrowed, her hands still moving in complex patterns. "Don't stop. Keep your focus. Don't let it breach."

Holly swallowed hard as she poured more of her magic into the spell. Fatigue crept in. The air crackled with energy, the barrier humming with visible power as they fought to keep the dark force at bay.

But the dark magic wasn't giving up. It pressed harder, pulsing like a living thing, trying to break through the protective barrier they had woven.

Demetrius shifted so that he was between the women and the door, his eyes fixed on the swirling force outside. "It's getting stronger."

Holly's pulse inched higher, her magic faltering for just a moment before she regained control. She was tired, but she knew she couldn't stop. "We need to hold it. Just a little longer."

The dark magic pulsed again, stronger this time, and Holly could feel the barrier weakening. She felt something else, too. As if part of her might snap right along with it. She refused to accept that even as the shadows outside seemed to grow larger, more solid, like they might be about to break free.

"Morgana!" Holly shouted, panic rising in her chest. Her arms were heavy from so much casting, and her spirit sagged.

But before Morgana could respond, the dark magic surged forward, slamming into the barrier with a force that shook the entire cabin and knocked Demetrius back.

The barrier shattered, splinters of light and magic sparking in the night air. Hexi and Moonshadow hissed and yowled before running for the bedroom.

Then the darkness rushed in.

The moment the barrier shattered, the air in the cabin turned freezing, as if the very life had been sucked out of the room. The door buckled but for the moment, held.

Holly's heart pounded in her chest, and her hands tingled with the remnants of her magic, but it wasn't enough to stop the darkness that surged in like a tidal wave.

"Morgana!" Holly shouted, every inch of her being alight with panic. "Demetrius!"

Alarm danced in Morgana's blue-violet eyes, her hands still moving in an attempt to salvage the remnants of the spell. But it was too late. The dark energy that had been pressing against the barrier for so long had broken free, and now it was inside, twisting and coiling around the room like a living shadow.

Demetrius sprang into action, stepping in front of Holly as the swirling darkness closed in around them. His eyes flashed a silvery gray, and for a moment, Holly caught a glimpse of the ancient, powerful being that lived within him. He wasn't just a broody, angsty vampire; he was a force of nature when he needed to be.

"Holly, get back," Demetrius growled, his voice low

and commanding, his body a shield between her and the door.

But Holly couldn't move. Her eyes were locked on the sinister tendrils of magic that slithered under the door and across the hardwood, creeping toward her and Morgana with ominous intent.

Morgana's voice cut through the howling wind and the rattling of the cabin walls. "This is it—the magic I warned you about. We need to contain it, now!"

Holly shoved down her trepidation and forced herself into action. The dark magic felt cold and wrong, like it didn't belong in this world. It wasn't just ancient—it was malevolent, and it was *hungry*.

With a surge of determination, Holly ignored her exhaustion, raised her hands, and began to weave another spell, knitting threads of magic the way she did yarn. Her magic flared to life, sparking at her fingertips as she focused on creating a containment field. Morgana joined in, their powers intertwining, but the darkness was fast—too fast.

Demetrius stepped forward, his fangs bared in a way that made Holly shiver. He was terrifying, and she was overjoyed they were on the same side. His muscles coiled as he prepared to fight the shadowy force. "This thing is going to keep coming. We have to stop it."

"We're trying," Holly assured him.

The shadows twisted and shifted, forming into a grotesque shape that loomed over them, its dark form barely recognizable as human. It was as if the magic itself had taken on a life of its own, pulling energy from the very air around them. Its eyes, if they could even be called that, glowed with a sickly green light, and a low, guttural hiss filled the cabin.

"That must be the ghost of Christmas never," Holly whispered, her voice tight with fear as she tried to pour more magic into the spell. She felt her strength waning, the energy required to hold back the darkness draining her faster than she'd ever experienced.

The shadowy figure let out a high-pitched wail, and with a sudden burst of speed, it lunged toward them. Holly's heart lurched into her throat, and she instinctively threw up a secondary protective wall of magic, but the creature slammed into it with a force that sent her stumbling backward.

Demetrius caught her before she hit the ground, his vampire speed impressive. His touch was cold but steady, the contact giving her something solid to cling to in the chaos of the moment.

"We need to push it back," Demetrius said, his voice low and controlled. "It's feeding off the energy in the room."

Morgana's eyes were narrowed in concentration, her hands still weaving spells as fast as she could. "It's ancient magic, and it's been waiting to be unleashed. We have to force it back into the forest. That's our only hope of containing it. There's enough magic there to strengthen our spells."

Holly gritted her teeth, getting back to her feet with

Demetrius's help. She wasn't going to let this thing win, not here, not in her cabin. She could feel her magic burning inside her, but it was fragile, like a candle about to go out.

"We can't let it spread into town," Holly said, filled with new determination. "If it gets past us, if it gets down the road, Nocturne Falls is in danger, as is everyone who lives there. That *cannot* happen."

Something dark and dangerous glinted in Demetrius's gaze as he stared down the shadowy figure. "Then we'll make sure it doesn't."

Without another word, Demetrius lunged at the dark mass, his speed almost impossible to follow. In an instant, he was a blur of motion, his hands gripping the shadowy tendrils of magic as he tried to wrestle the creature away from Holly and Morgana.

The shadow hissed, twisting violently in Demetrius's grip, but he held firm, his fangs flashing as he snarled. Holly could see the strain on his face, the effort it took to contain something that was so clearly unnatural, so deeply malicious.

Holly's hands shook as she poured the last of her magic into the containment field. She could feel the spell taking hold, but it wasn't enough. The darkness was too strong, too ancient. She needed something more—something powerful.

"Holly!" Morgana shouted, her voice snapping Holly back to the present. "Use your family's magic. You're the only one who can finish this!"

Every doubt she'd ever had about her magic and her abilities came rushing back. Her family's magic was ancient, protective, built to guard against threats like this. But she had never used it like this before. She'd always been too afraid to try. What if she couldn't control it? What if it wasn't enough?

It didn't matter what the answers were. She didn't have a choice. She'd never be able to live with herself if she didn't try.

With a deep breath, Holly closed her eyes and reached deep within, calling on the magic that had been passed down through her family for generations. It stirred inside her, warm and familiar, an old friend, even if it was one she didn't know as well as she would have liked. The power surged through her, charging into her veins with a bright, protective energy.

When she opened her eyes, her hands glowed with a pale, peachy light—the color of her family's magic. She could feel the strength of it, the way it pulsed with life, with love, with protection. It was everything she needed to fight back the darkness. A sense of calm swept through her as though she'd been lifted above the chaos.

"Demetrius, hold on," Holly said in a clear voice that somehow carried above the howling wind and the wailing darkness.

Demetrius nodded, his grip tightening on the shadowy figure as Holly stepped forward, her hands glowing brighter with each passing second.

Holly raised her hands, focusing all her energy on the

dark figure. Her magic surged forward, wrapping around the creature like a net, pulling it back, forcing it out the door, away from the cabin, and toward the forest where it belonged.

The shadow screamed in protest, writhing and twisting as Holly's magic wrapped it tighter and tighter. She still didn't let up, even though her limbs began to shake. She pushed harder, forcing it back, inch by inch, until finally, with a piercing cry, the shadowy figure was sucked back into the darkness of the forest, disappearing into the trees like smoke.

The silence that followed was deafening.

Holly collapsed to her knees, the glow of her magic fading as exhaustion washed over her. She sank lower until her cheek pressed against the hardwood. Her heart began to calm, but her breath still came in short gasps. The air in the cabin remained cold, but the oppressive darkness was gone.

Demetrius shut the door, then was at her side, his hands lifting her, scooping her into his arms. "Holly, are you all right? Say something."

Holly nodded, though her body felt like it had been hit by a freight train. "I—I think so."

Morgana approached, her face pale but determined. "You are very powerful. That was ... impressive. You contained it."

Holly looked up at Morgana, her voice weak. She'd never felt so drained in her life. "Is it gone? For good?"

Morgana shook her head. "Not gone. But contained.

We pushed it back into the forest. It's weaker now, but it's not defeated. We'll need to keep an eye on it."

Holly's heart sank. So it wasn't over. The dark magic was still out there, lurking in the woods, waiting for another chance to break free. But at least for now, they had stopped it.

She took a deep breath, her hands still trembling. She didn't like the idea of keeping an eye on it, but she was tired. "We'll deal with it when it comes. But right now, I need to rest."

"Of course," Morgana said. "We both do."

"I can stand," Holly told Demetrius.

He put her on her feet, his arm around her waist to support her, his touch gentle. "You've earned the rest, that's for sure."

As Holly leaned against him, the fire crackling softly in the hearth, she realized something. For the first time in a long time, she wasn't facing life alone. She had Morgana, who, despite her mysterious ways, had come through. And she had Demetrius, her once questionable vampire neighbor, who'd not only stood by her side through it all but had put himself in danger on her behalf.

Together, they had faced the darkness.

And together, they would face whatever came next.

The following morning, the world outside the cabin was still and silent, blanketed in the pure white of fresh snow that was still falling. Holly stood at the living room window, her breath fogging up the glass as she gazed out at the peaceful scene. She sipped her coffee, made by Demetrius.

It was hard to believe that just hours ago, dark magic had surged through the same forest, threatening to overtake everything in its path, probably intent on killing them and doing who knew what to the town below. Now, the trees stood tall and quiet, as if the supernatural storm had never happened.

But Holly knew better.

Her muscles ached from the magic she had wielded, and lingering questions filled her mind. The dark magic was contained for now, but it wasn't gone. Whatever had been unleashed was still out there, lurking in the shadows of the forest, waiting for its next chance. She could feel it, a low hum at the back of her consciousness, like the echo of something ancient and dangerous.

The barrier would have to be rebuilt, but not today. Today she needed to rest.

Demetrius, standing beside her, seemed to sense it

too. His eyes scanned the horizon for any sign of movement, his body tense as if ready to spring into action at the slightest provocation. Despite the calm outside, neither of them could shake the feeling that something was still brewing.

"You should sit down," Demetrius said, his voice low and steady, though his concern was clear. "I'm sure you still need rest."

Holly shook her head, her hands tightening around the mug of coffee she held. "I'm fine. Just ... trying to process everything." Even so, she moved to her armchair and sat, relaxing in the warmth of the fire.

Demetrius's gaze softened, and for a moment, Holly allowed herself to take in his presence. He had been so constant, so steady throughout all of this—her rock in the middle of a storm. His stoic demeanor never wavered.

The truth was, the quiet strength in the way he stood by her, offering support without asking for anything in return, had caused her to see him in a new light. The kind of light that made her want him around all the time.

Probably too much to expect from a man like him. A wealthy vampire who made the world his home.

"You saved the town last night," Demetrius said quietly, his gaze meeting hers. He sat in the other armchair.

Holly quickly shook her head. "*We* saved the town."

Demetrius's faint smile disappeared as quickly as it arrived. "It was you. And Morgana. But it was mostly you."

"Trust me, you helped more than you realize."

"If I did, then I'm glad. But that thing isn't gone, Holly. You know that as well as I do."

Holly nodded, her chest tightening with the truth of his words. "Yeah, I know. We bought ourselves some time, but it'll be back. And when it comes, we'll need to be ready."

Demetrius's expression darkened. "I didn't want to admit it, but Morgana's right—it's feeding off something. It wasn't just trying to escape; it was growing, getting stronger. We have to find out what's driving it."

Holly bit her lip, her mind racing. The dark magic had been waiting for something—something powerful enough to trigger it. But what? Nocturne Falls was home to all sorts of supernatural creatures, but ancient dark magic wasn't part of anyone's usual holiday festivities. Or *any* festivities.

That kind of thing was generally frowned upon in Nocturne Falls.

"Morgana's not telling us everything." Holly sighed, her own reluctance in admitting that hard to take. "She knows more about this magic than she's letting on."

Demetrius nodded in agreement. "She does. I still don't think I trust her, despite her help last night. I just don't know."

Holly sighed, leaning back against the chair. "Trusting Morgana feels like walking on thin ice—one wrong step, and we could come crashing down. But she did help us fight off the dark magic, and for now, that might have to be enough." Holly just hoped it stayed that way.

"It might have to be," he said.

Just then, the sound of footsteps coming up the porch steps caught their attention. The doorknob turned and the door swung open, revealing Morgana, her expression as unreadable as ever, though there was a definite stiffness to her posture. Her blue-violet eyes flicked between Holly and Demetrius, assessing them both.

"We need to talk," Morgana said, her voice clipped. "The dark magic isn't finished."

Holly sighed, setting down her mug and giving the older woman a hard look. "So you said. Listen, I get that you're a pretty powerful witch, but maybe knock instead of using your magic."

"My apologies." Morgana pursed her lips. "I thought you wanted to save the town."

Demetrius sighed loudly. "Saving the town and wanting some common courtesy are not contradictory ideals."

Holly smirked. "Come in, Morgana. Have you learned anything new about this malevolent force? Like why it's here? Or what triggered it?"

Morgana stepped inside and closed the door, again using magic. Her gaze lingered on Holly for a moment, then she took a seat on the couch, staying to the end opposite of Moonshadow, who was nesting in the blankets again. "Just what I've told you. It's older than this town. Older than any of us in it. I've been tracking it for years, watching it slowly gather strength. That's how I ended up here. I followed it. Something disturbed it recently, though I still don't know what. All I know is that it's connected to the land itself."

Holly frowned. "Connected to the land how?"

Morgana's fingers twitched slightly, as if she were still caught up in the remnants of last night's magic. "This place—Nocturne Falls—it's a hub for supernatural energy. You must know that. Because of Alice Bishop, the magic that flows through this town is old, far older than most of the creatures who live here."

"Then why don't we get Alice to help?" Holly suggested.

"Because Alice and all the Ellinghams are gone to France for Christmas. They won't be back until after the New Year," Morgana answered.

"Oh." Holly squinted. "Actually, I think I remember hearing that."

"We have to do something," Morgana said. "The town's energy increases every year, and the dark magic is feeding off it."

Demetrius's eyes narrowed. "Why now?"

Morgana's lips pressed into a narrow line. "I'm not sure. It could be something as simple as a disturbance in the magical balance. Or it could be something far more intentional."

That made Holly think. "Someone triggered this?"

Morgana didn't answer immediately, her gaze distant, as if she were piecing together a puzzle that had too many missing pieces. "It's possible. I've felt stirrings of magic, whispers in the wind, but nothing concrete. Whoever—or whatever—caused this has been careful."

Holly's thoughts tumbled over each other. She'd been expecting a peaceful holiday in her cabin, and now she was tangled in something far more dangerous. Dark magic, ancient forces, and now the possibility that someone was doing all this on purpose?

Maybe she should have gone to her brother's, but visits there just reminded her that she was not married with kids. Something her parents mostly avoided mentioning, but she knew it was on their minds.

Enough of that. She had troubles of her own to deal with.

"Who would do this?" Holly asked, her voice tight with frustration. "And why now, at Christmastime?"

Morgana's gaze landed on Holly, her eyes cold and calculating. "Quite possibly because the Ellinghams and Alice are gone. It's the perfect opportunity. But there are plenty of beings in this world who thrive on chaos. Dark magic is tempting—it promises power even though it comes with a high price. It's possible someone in this town has been dabbling in something they don't fully understand."

Demetrius crossed his arms, his expression dark. "Then we find them and we get to the bottom of this."

Holly nodded, determination filling her. "I agree. We don't have a choice. If this magic keeps growing, it's going to tear through the barrier again—and next time, we might not be able to stop it. Which reminds me, the barrier still needs to be rebuilt."

Demetrius looked at her. "You need to rest."

"I'll be all right." She couldn't say the words out loud, but having him around gave her energy. She'd get through this so long as he was by her side.

"There is no time to rest." Morgana's gaze remained steady, but Holly couldn't help the nagging feeling that there was still more the witch wasn't telling them.

At least for now, they had a plan. Find the source of the disturbance, figure out what had triggered the dark magic, and stop it before it was too late.

Demetrius straightened, his gaze going to the windows again. "We have to start talking to the locals. If anyone's been messing with magic, someone will have noticed."

Morgana nodded, though her expression remained guarded. "I'll search the outskirts of town, see if I can pick up any traces of dark energy. But be careful who you trust. Not everyone in Nocturne Falls is as harmless as they seem."

"Let me ask Flavia to reach out to the coven, see if they've heard anything else." Holly forced herself to stay calm, but it was hard. They were up against something ancient and powerful, but thankfully, they weren't powerless. They had magic, and they had each other.

"That would be good," Morgana said, getting up. "If I find anything, I'll tell you when I return." She left, slipping out of the cabin quietly.

Holly reached for her phone and quickly sent Flavia a text with an update about what was going on, asking her to see what she could find out.

With that done, Holly turned to Demetrius, her spirit heavy with the weight of everything they had to do.

"I sent Flavia a text," Holly said, doing her best to keep her mood up. "What do we do next?"

Demetrius met her gaze, a spark of something in his eyes—something fierce and unwavering. "We find out who's been playing with magic. And we stop them."

"Easier said than done."

Holly took a deep breath. There were plenty of magical beings in Nocturne Falls, any one of whom could be involved in whatever had triggered the dark magic. But where to begin? A thought came to her.

"What about Howler's? The woman who owns it, Bridget Merrow, is a werewolf and about as well connected as anyone in town. I mean, one of her brothers is the sheriff, and the other one's the fire chief," Holly said. "If anyone's heard rumors about dark magic, it's her."

Demetrius nodded. "That's a great idea. We can talk to her and maybe get some lunch while we're there. The sooner we get answers, the better."

"Lunch?" Holly looked at the time. It was later than she'd thought.

They got ready to leave, and as they stepped out into the cold air to get in his SUV, Holly couldn't help but feel a flash of happiness. Demetrius was beside her, the snow-covered trees shimmered in the soft light of the sun, and for a moment, everything felt calm. Peaceful.

Of course, she knew better than to trust the calm. There was darkness lurking just beneath the surface.

She just hoped they weren't running out of time to stop it.

The drive into town felt longer than before, maybe because there was so much on Demetrius's mind. Mostly it was Holly and his concern for her. It pressed down on him like a weight, and he had a feeling Holly could sense it too.

He tried to relax, but his whole body was rigid with worry. He couldn't stop himself from scanning their surroundings as if he expected the shadows between the trees to come alive. Maybe they would. Who knew what this ancient magic was capable of?

The snowfall had finally eased, leaving a fresh blanket of snow on the ground that crunched beneath the SUV's tires as they headed for Howler's.

The town still looked as enchanted as ever with snow-covered rooftops, twinkling holiday lights, and the scent of woodsmoke lingering in the crisp winter air. But something sinister lurked beneath the festive surface. Something no one else knew about.

It made Demetrius look at everything differently. Could they save the town? They had to. Whatever it took. This was Holly's home. And he was thinking about making it his, too. His permanent home. For that to happen, he had to protect it.

Demetrius stayed quiet as he drove, but a multitude of unanswered questions swirled through his mind. What was the power source of the darkness they were facing? How much stronger could it get? Who was behind it? He felt like a coiled spring ready to snap at the first sign of danger.

"What do you think we'll find?" Holly asked, her voice barely above a whisper as he turned onto Main Street.

His gaze remained fixed ahead. The roads had been plowed, but they were icy in spots. The last thing they needed was to get into an accident. "I have no idea. But if someone in town is responsible for this, we should be able to find out soon enough."

Holly nodded, a frown on her face and a hand on her stomach.

He didn't like that she was so upset, but he understood. The idea that someone in Nocturne Falls—someone they might know, someone who knew better—could be dabbling in dark magic was unsettling.

The town was built on the idea of supernatural harmony, a place where witches, vampires, and all sorts of magical beings coexisted peacefully. The thought that someone could be using that harmony to hide something dangerous made his skin crawl. He could only imagine what it was doing to her.

He parked just outside of Howler's. Wasn't hard to get a good spot, as the town still seemed pretty quiet. No doubt most people were staying in, getting ready for Christmas and spending time with their families.

They got out and walked into the restaurant. He'd only been here once before, in the very early days of his family's arrival here, but it hadn't changed. The only real difference was how empty the place was. Only three tables had customers, with two more seated at one end of the bar. Those two were being served by a smiling redhead in a leopard-and-black Santa hat.

The faint smell of wolf, something he alone probably picked up on, permeated the place. He leaned toward Holly. "Is that Bridget behind the bar?"

Holly nodded. "It is."

"Then let's sit there to eat so we can talk to her."

"Good idea."

They took seats at the opposite end of the bar from the other two patrons to give themselves some privacy.

Bridget approached with menus. "Hello, brave people. Nice to see the snow hasn't kept everyone away. What can I get you to drink?"

"Coke?" Holly said.

"Coffee," Demetrius said. "Black."

"Coming right up. We only have one special for lunch today. Christmas dinner. Roast turkey, stuffing, green bean casserole, mashed potatoes with gravy, candied sweet potatoes, and a side of cranberry sauce. We also have pumpkin pie for dessert. Be right back with those drinks."

She left, and Demetrius put his menu down. "The special works for me."

"Me, too." Holly let out a little sigh. "I hope she knows something."

"So do I."

Bridget returned with the beverages. "Need a few more minutes?"

Holly shook her head. "The special sounds great."

"Same here," Demetrius said.

"Good choice."

Holly offered a small smile as she handed over her menu. "There is one other thing."

"Oh?" Bridget stayed put.

"This is a strange request," Holly started. "But have you heard anyone talking about dabbling in dark magic lately? Or have any reason to believe someone might be? I'm Holly Winters. My family built the barrier that—"

"Protects the Voss mansion," Bridget finished, her gaze on Demetrius.

"It's not a mansion," he corrected her.

Bridget snorted. "Um, yes, it is. It looks like a ski lodge, except it's a private home. I'd say it's a mansion." Her amusement disappeared as her attention returned to Holly. "What's going on now?"

Demetrius let Holly explain, and she did in just a few sentences, telling Bridget about the barrier, the strange ripple, and everything that had happened with Morgana.

Bridget's concern was plainly visible on her face. "What a time for Alice and all the Ellinghams to be out of town."

"We can handle it," Holly assured her. "But getting a little more information would help a lot. We're dealing with something dark. There's ancient magic stirring in the woods—dangerous magic. And we think someone in town is responsible. Or they might have triggered it unknowingly. Anyway, if we could find out who that person is ..."

Bridget's eyes widened slightly, her expression turning serious. "You're sure it's dark magic and not just some weird fluctuation?"

Demetrius remained calm but firm. "Positive. We've already had a run-in with it, and it's not done yet."

Bridget chewed her bottom lip, her eyes shifting to the two customers at the other end before answering. "I've heard whispers—rumors, mostly—but nothing concrete. A couple of the local witches were in for lunch last week, and I overhead them talking about feeling strange energy shifts lately, but no one's come forward about using dark magic. Not to me, anyway. Most people in town know better than to mess with forces like that."

"As they should," Holly said.

Demetrius sighed, his frustration building. He had hoped for more, something tangible that could point them in the right direction. "Do you have any idea who might be involved? Anyone who's been asking about old magic? Family magic?"

Bridget hesitated for a moment, then nodded. "Look, I don't like to spread rumors, but there is someone. A newcomer. She's been coming in here every night for dinner. Name's Neeva. She always sits alone and always has a book with her. Usually some kind of old book that looks very much like a grimoire. She didn't seem dangerous, though. Just ... odd. But odd is pretty normal is this town."

"True," Demetrius said, thrilled they were getting somewhere. "Anything else you can remember? Like the titles of any of the books? Anything else you might have overheard?"

Bridget took a deep breath, eyes narrowing. "Now that you mention it, I think one of the books might have been about binding spells or boundary spells. I can't really remember. I only saw the front cover in passing. Could be nothing, but it stood out to me."

Next to him, Holly's pulse quickened.

Demetrius smiled at Bridget. "That's been really helpful. Thanks. Can't wait to try that special."

Bridget nodded. "Glad to help. I'll get those orders in right now."

Holly turned to him as Bridget walked away. "Binding spells are a type of magic used to lock away or contain something. That fits with what Morgana had said about the dark magic being dormant for centuries, waiting for something to release it. If this Neeva is looking into binding spells, she might know about the dark magic that's been awakened, too."

He nodded. "Makes sense. But she might know about it because she's the one who released it."

When Bridget returned with their meals, Demetrius wasted no time. "Where can we find Neeva? We need to talk to her."

"She lives at 19 Broomstick Lane," Bridget replied.

"Appropriate," Demetrius muttered.

"I only know that because she's gotten deliveries from us. But listen, be careful if you go see her. I don't know what she's up to or what she's capable of, but if she's been dabbling in dark magic ... well, you know better than I do what that could mean."

Holly gave a quick, uneasy nod. "I do. Thanks, Bridget. We'll be careful."

Bridget hesitated. "You know, my brother's the sheriff. If you wanted, I could talk to him. Maybe see if he could help?"

"I appreciate the offer, but what can he do without proof?" Demetrius said. "And it's not like a crime has been committed. That we know about."

"Yeah, true," Bridget said. "Well, let me know if anything changes. And enjoy your lunch."

They ate quickly, both driven by the unspoken agreement that they needed to find this Neeva as soon as they could. Demetrius dropped a hundred-dollar bill on the bar, told Bridget to keep the change, and with a wave of thanks, they headed outside.

As they stepped back into the cold and went to the car, Demetrius worked through the possibilities. Could Neeva really be the one responsible for unleashing the dark magic? Or was she just another pawn in whatever was happening? Either way, they had to find out—and soon.

Demetrius walked around and opened Holly's door.

"Thanks. You okay? You seem tense." She wrinkled her nose. "Tenser than usual."

"I'm fine. Just ..." He sighed. "The closer we get to this thing, the more dangerous it feels. This woman, Neeva, she's either involved or knows something about the dark magic. Either way, we could be headed into trouble."

Holly nodded, her breath forming soft clouds in the frigid air. "I get that, but I don't totally agree. If she's been researching binding spells, maybe she didn't mean to release the magic. Maybe she was trying to control it. And now she wants to fix whatever she did accidentally."

"Or maybe she knew exactly what she was doing," Demetrius replied darkly.

Holly's expression twisted at his words. "Maybe. But it's one thing to inadvertently unleash something dangerous. It was another thing entirely to do it on purpose."

"And we won't know until we confront her." With a frustrated grunt, Demetrius shut Holly's door and went around to get behind the wheel.

As they made their way toward Broomstick Lane, they passed houses decorated with evergreen boughs and festive ornaments, wreaths on the front doors, and snowmen in the front yards. Some were still being built by children bundled up against the cold. Smoke drifted up from nearly every chimney.

19 Broomstick Lane came into view, nestled between two larger homes, its roof dusted with snow and smoke curling lazily from the chimney. The little blue and white house looked quaint and peaceful, but Demetrius's instincts told him looks weren't everything. They had no idea about the woman inside or what her intentions were.

Especially where Holly was concerned, and that bothered him for reasons he dared not spend too much time thinking about.

Demetrius's eyes narrowed as they approached the door. "Stay behind me," he grumbled. "She could be dangerous."

"I am a witch, you know. I'm not without skills. As you've seen," Holly said.

"I know, but this woman is an unknown. If she's going to do something, let me take the brunt of it."

Holly looked like she wanted to protest. Instead, she nodded, standing close behind him as he knocked on the door, positioning himself so that he was ready for anything.

For a moment, there was silence. Then the door creaked open, revealing a woman who looked to be in her fifties, her dark blond hair tied back in a low ponytail. Her eyes—honey gold—wavered between Holly and Demetrius with a hint of suspicion.

"Can I help you?" the woman—Neeva, Demetrius presumed—asked, her voice edged with wariness.

"We're here to ask you a few questions," Demetrius said, trying to look as nonthreatening as possible. Not something he had a lot of experience with.

Neeva's gaze narrowed slightly. "What kind of questions?"

Holly stepped forward, her voice gentle but determined. "We know you've been researching binding spells. We need to know why. There's dark magic stirring in the woods, and we think you might know something about it."

For a brief moment, something shone in Neeva's eyes —fear, maybe, or guilt. But it was gone as quickly as it had appeared, replaced by a mask of indifference.

"I don't know what you're talking about," Neeva said, her tone cold and dismissive. "Now, if you'll excuse me—"

But Demetrius wasn't having it. His hand shot out, catching the door before she could close it. "We're not leaving until we get answers."

Neeva's eyes flashed with anger, but Demetrius could see the truth in them—she *did* know something. And she was hiding it.

"Look," Holly said in a tone that brooked no argument. "We're not here to accuse you of anything. But something dangerous has been unleashed, and if we don't stop it, people are going to get hurt. We just need to know what you know."

Neeva hesitated, looking at the two of them like she was sizing them up for potential danger. For a moment,

Demetrius thought she might attempt to slam the door in their faces, but then Neeva let out a long, shaky breath.

"Fine," she muttered, stepping back to let them in. "But I don't know how much help I'll be."

Demetrius went in first and had a quick look around as Holly followed. The house was small and nicely furnished, with shelves lined with jars of herbs and old books. A fire crackled softly in the hearth, casting a warm glow over the room, but even to him, the air felt heavy, thick with the residue of magic.

Neeva moved to the small table in the center of the room and sat down, her hands fidgeting nervously against the table's scarred surface. "I didn't mean for this to happen."

Holly's eyes widened. "What do you mean?"

Neeva sighed, her eyes filled with regret. "I was researching binding spells to try and contain something —an old power I sensed in the woods. I didn't think it was dangerous at first, but the more I worked on it, the more it resisted. And then ..." She looked away.

"Then what?" Demetrius asked.

Neeva swallowed. "I lost control."

Holly looked ill. "You released it?"

Neeva nodded, her voice barely a whisper. "I thought I could contain it, but it's stronger than I realized. Now it's out there, and I don't know how to stop it. Nothing I've read seems capable of helping. I don't know how to contain it again."

Demetrius's jaw tightened as anger surged through him. "Why didn't you tell anyone?"

Neeva looked down at her hands, guilt written all over her face. "I was afraid. I didn't want anyone to know I'd messed with something so powerful. I thought if I could fix it on my own, no one would have to know."

Holly exchanged a glance with Demetrius, and the look said it all.

Neeva had unleashed the dark magic, and now it was up to them to stop it. But he wasn't sure they could do it alone. They shouldn't have to. Not if it meant Holly would be in danger.

"You're going to help us fix this," Holly said. Demetrius was surprised but proud of her for standing strong. "You know the magic better than anyone. We need your help to stop it."

Neeva looked up, fear and determination battling in her eyes. "I'll help. But we need to act fast. It's getting stronger every day."

"We know," Demetrius said. "Which is why we can't waste any more time. You need to come with us, and we need to take care of this immediately."

Clearly resigned, Neeva got up and started to gather her things.

As they left the house and stepped outside, Demetrius wondered if Neeva really could help them. At least they'd found the source of the disturbance, but the real battle was just beginning. The dark magic was growing, and if they didn't stop it soon, Nocturne Falls would be swallowed by the darkness.

Demetrius wasn't sure their combined powers would be enough, but what really worried him was the toll it was going to take on Holly.

He couldn't deny he'd started to care about her. And to him, that was almost more frightening than what waited for them in the forest.

Demetrius said nothing on the drive back to the cabin, so Holly let him be. Neeva trailed them in her own car, and every time Holly glanced in the side mirror, Neeva looked more worried.

Holly felt for her, but this was her doing. The revelation of her role in releasing the dark magic weighed on all of them, but they didn't have the time or luxury to dwell. They had to act. The darkness was growing stronger, and it wasn't going to wait for them to sort through their emotions.

Snow started to fall in delicate, lazy patterns, coating the world around them in a peaceful stillness that belied the danger lurking just beyond the tree line. The sky had turned a soft gray, and Holly could feel the temperature dropping despite the SUV's warm interior. Maybe it was the weight of what was to come.

Demetrius kept his eyes on the road, silent and focused, his expression unreadable, as it so often was. But Holly had grown to sense the subtle shifts in his mood—the tension in his posture, the way his eyes skimmed the trees more often than usual. He was on high alert, and that told her everything she needed to know.

Neeva, on the other hand, looked like a mess of

nerves. Holly could practically feel the guilt radiating off of her through the vehicles. Holly didn't know what to make of her yet. Neeva had messed up—there was no doubt about that—but the fear and regret in her eyes confirmed what Neeva had said. She hadn't meant for any of this to happen.

That was no excuse for keeping it a secret. Not when it was the kind of magic that could wipe out the town.

They reached the cabin as the light was starting to fade, the snow-covered roof and glowing windows making the place look almost idyllic. It was hard to believe that a battle was brewing in the woods beyond, one that could change everything if they didn't stop it in time.

Demetrius parked, Neeva behind him, and as the three went inside, the warmth of the embers in the fireplace greeted them. But to Holly, the air felt tense, charged with the leftover energy from the barrier spells and the lingering presence of the dark magic they'd fought the night before.

Hexi, lounging on the hearth rug, lifted his head and gave a moody meow at their entrance, as if to say, *What took you so long?*

Moonshadow was curled up in one of the armchairs, her eyes lazily watching Neeva, but Holly saw a new alertness in both the animals. The cats knew something was up. Even they could feel the shift in the energy around them.

"Nice place," Neeva said. "Very homey."

"Thanks," Holly answered.

Demetrius closed the door behind them and turned to Neeva with an expectant look. "You said you'd help. So where do we start?"

Neeva hesitated, wringing her hands as she stood in the center of the room. "I ... I'm not sure. The magic I was working with was older than anything I've ever encountered. I thought I could bind it and contain it, but it fought back. I've never experienced that before. It was almost like it had a will of its own."

Holly exchanged a glance with Demetrius. The idea that the dark magic was sentient, that it had its own purpose, sent a chill down her spine. "You said it's connected to the land," Holly said, pacing near the fire. "Do you think it's something that's been lying dormant for centuries then?"

Neeva nodded, her eyes wide with fear. "Yes. I believe it's tied to the original magic of this place, the magic that's always existed here, which is probably why the Ellinghams chose to buy this town. When I first came to Nocturne Falls, I felt the pull of it—the raw energy in the earth. But I didn't realize how deep it went until it was too late."

Demetrius frowned, his arms crossed over his chest. "Are you saying the town itself is connected to this darkness? Because that's a pretty serious claim."

One they'd heard from Morgana, which made Holly think the old witch had been telling the truth.

"I know, but it's what I think," Neeva replied, her voice wavering. "This place draws supernatural beings because of the protection this town offers. But the magic that Alice Bishop put into place—I think it's seeped into the ground and gone beneath the surface. And that magic is what's awoken the existing magic. There's something dark down there. Something that's using Alice's good magic to power itself back to life. I didn't realize it at first, but when I started working with the binding spells, I tapped into something old and dangerous."

Holly's mind started putting the pieces into place. Nocturne Falls had been a safe haven for magical creatures ever since Alice had bespelled the water of the falls to keep tourists from realizing what they were really seeing, but that safety had come a cost no one could have guessed. The dark magic Neeva had released wasn't just something she'd done by accident—it had been waiting for the right moment, for the right trigger, to break free.

Neeva had just provided it.

"We need to rebuild the barrier. I don't see any other way," Holly said as fear gnawed at her insides. "But this time, it won't be enough to just patch it up and hope for the best. We first need to find the source of the dark magic, where it's strongest, and contain it at the root."

Demetrius didn't look happy. "The forest."

Holly nodded. "That's where the magic is coming from. If we can get to the heart of it, we might be able to cut it off before it spreads any further."

Neeva hugged her arms around her body. "The forest is where the magic is strongest. But it's also where it's most dangerous. If we go in unprepared, we could be walking right into a trap. We're magical beings. This ancient entity could see us as more fuel for its fire. I do *not* want to get absorbed into it."

"None of us do." A muscle twitched in Demetrius's jaw. "But we don't have a choice. If we don't stop it now, the entire town is at risk. Every supernatural being who lives here is at risk."

Holly could feel the tension in the room brought on by the weight of the decision they were about to make. Going into the forest was a gamble, but staying here, waiting for the dark magic to break through again, was an even bigger one. One they could only lose. She took a deep breath, gathering her strength.

"We're not going in blind," Holly said, her resolve firm. "We'll prepare as much as we can. Reinforce the barrier around the cabin, gather our magic, and go in with a plan."

Neeva nodded, though her hands still trembled slightly. "I'll help. I owe it to you all—and to the town—to fix what I've done."

Demetrius watched Neeva with an almost understanding gaze. "You made a mistake, but you're here now. We'll fix it together."

Holly felt a swell of something warm in her chest at his words. Demetrius might be a brooding vampire most of the time, but he had a way of making people feel seen and understood. Even Neeva, who had caused so much trouble, was being given a second chance.

"Let's get started," Holly said, turning toward the table where her magical supplies were laid out. "We don't have much time."

Demetrius moved closer to her. "Should you call in reinforcements?"

"Like Morgana?"

"Like anyone. You know other witches in this town. What about Flavia?"

Holly shook her head. "I don't know. It's a lot to ask around Christmastime, and it's my family's magic that's being targeted. None of them can really help with that the way I can."

"Just think about it."

"I will," she promised.

The next few hours were a blur of preparation. Holly, Demetrius, and Neeva worked together to gather the necessary supplies—crystals, herbs, candles, salt, iron, and anything else they could use to strengthen the barrier and protect themselves from the dark magic.

The cats lounged around and focused on being cats.

Holly, somewhat reluctantly, called Flavia, updated her on what was going on without overly stressing the part about the town possibly being in danger, and asked if she would be willing to help as backup, should they need it. Which she said they probably wouldn't.

Not only did Flavia seem to see right through Holly's attempt to downplay things, but she agreed to help and promised to bring anyone else who might be interested, including Morgana.

Demetrius tried to hide how pleased that made him, but Holly wasn't fooled by his attempt to pretend otherwise.

Flavia, her braids tucked under a cozy knitted cap, showed up with Charisma Williams, another talented witch. Charisma, with her dark brunette bob and whiskey-brown eyes was so pretty and so stylishly dressed in winter white, she made Holly look twice.

Holly immediately thanked them for coming, introduced them to Neeva, and then they all got to work setting up a ward around the cabin's exterior.

She got Flavia alone. "Where's Morgana?"

"I don't have a clue. Her place was empty, and her car was gone. All I can think of is that she decided this was too much for her and took off."

Holly frowned. "So much for her helping."

"Hey," Flavia said. "If she didn't think she could handle it, then it's better not to have her here. Hesitant magic can cause a lot of trouble, something I don't think you need right now."

"True, I don't." None of them did. With a quick smile for her friend, Holly got back to work, doing her best to ignore the cold. Her hands moved on autopilot as she arranged her part of the protective circle on top of the snow, her mind focused on the task before them and the enormity of getting it right.

Flavia and Charisma chanted softly as they added to their sections of the circle, putting their own magic into what they were doing. But Neeva did her part silently, the weight of her guilt still heavy in the air and very much visible on her face. Holly let her be. Whatever she was feeling was hers to deal with.

Not to mention, they needed her help now, and there would be time for apologies later. If they made it through this.

Demetrius stayed nearby like a sentinel, keeping watch as the sun began to sink behind the trees. The light filtering through the trees had turned a brilliant orange, giving everything around them a fiery glow. It was pretty, but the darkness was coming, and with it, the threat of the magic that had been released into the forest.

Holly finished and straightened, stretching her back, then went to find the other women. They were at the front of the cabin, all three of them eyeing Demetrius carefully. "I just finished. Are you guys done?"

Charisma tore her attention from Demetrius to answer Holly. "We are."

"Good," Holly said. "Then the perimeter is set." She wiped her hands on her jeans as she surveyed the circle of protection they'd created around the cabin. "It should hold while we're gone, but we need to move fast once we begin the containment spell."

"I agree," Demetrius said, his eyes scanning the tree line. "Fast is a good idea. This magic seems strongest at night, but that's also when we should be able to track it the easiest."

Holly rolled her shoulders, trying to loosen the tension she was feeling. They were about to walk into the heart of the darkness, but they had no other choice. If they didn't stop the magic at its source, it would consume everything in its path.

As the last light of day faded and the sky turned to a deep, inky blue speckled with a few stars, Holly pulled her gloves from her coat pocket and put them on. Her nerves seemed at the edge of her skin as she glanced up at Demetrius, who stood beside her, his presence as steady and reassuring as ever.

Neeva moved to the edge of the property, her eyes filled with both fear and determination as she gazed into the forest. "I'll lead the way," she said, a little hitch in her voice. "I know where the core of the magic is. But you'll need to be careful. It's unpredictable."

"We know that." Holly went up on the porch and grabbed the bag of magical supplies she'd packed. "Let's do this."

Together, the four of them followed Neeva into the cold forest, the weight of their mission heavy on their shoulders. The forest loomed around them, dim and foreboding, the trees bare, their branches stretching out like claws, waiting to pull them into the darkness.

But Holly wasn't afraid.

Not with Demetrius by her side.

And as they made their way into the forest, the soft crunch of snow beneath their feet, Holly focused on what she wanted to happen, not what she feared.

They were going to contain this dark magic. They were going to stop it. They were going to protect Nocturne Falls and everyone in it.

No matter what it took.

The towering trees stretched into the night sky as if trying to block out the stars. They were almost doing it, too. The deeper into the forest they went, the darker it got.

Holly's breath came in short, sharp pants as she followed behind Neeva, Charisma, and Flavia, her boots sinking deep into the snow with each step. The cold gnawed at her, biting through her coat and gloves, but it was nothing compared with the chill creeping up her spine.

This was it. They were heading straight into the heart of the dark magic, into the unknown. What awaited them was anyone's guess.

So maybe she'd lied to herself about not being afraid, because in truth, she was terrified but too stubborn to give in to her fears. She had to do this. She *would* do this. They all had to. The alternative was unacceptable.

Demetrius walked alongside her when the trees and brush didn't block his path, his head up, his eyes steely with determination. Like fear wasn't even a word in his vocabulary. Probably wasn't. Somehow, despite the heavy snow, his movements were swift and graceful. Undoubtedly a vampire thing.

Neeva led the way, her hands trembling slightly as she clutched the lantern she'd brought as part of her supplies. It cast a weak, wavering light over the forest floor, making the shadows dance as it swung. They seemed to close in around them, thicker and darker than they had any right to be.

Was that the magic at play? She could feel an unnatural energy thrumming in the air around them. It was getting stronger the deeper they went into the woods, like a low hum just at the edge of her consciousness, growing louder with each step.

The little hairs on the back of her neck lifted.

"How much farther?" Demetrius asked in a low growl as his eyes scanned the landscape around them. He most likely had the best night vision of all of them, something Holly trusted he was putting to good use. It was pretty reassuring to think he could see things a lot sooner than the rest of them.

Neeva didn't turn to look at him, her gaze fixed straight ahead as she kept walking. "We're close. I can feel it."

Charisma and Flavia both nodded in agreement.

Holly figured a person would have to be human *not* to feel it. Magic wafted through the night, ancient, twisted, and malevolent. It tripped across her skin and suffused the air, making her feel like she was wading through something as thick and sticky as tar. The trees around them seemed to shift and sway, even though there wasn't a breeze, and the shadows twisted into strange, unnatural shapes.

It was, in a word, creepy.

"Stay close," Demetrius said quietly, his gaze shifting to Holly as if sensing her growing unease.

"I'm right with you," Holly replied, her voice steadier than she felt. She glanced around, her breath misting in the frigid air. Every sound, every rustle of leaves or snap of a twig, made her jump. The forest was too quiet, too still, as if the very life of it had been drained away by the dark magic they were hunting.

Or maybe all that life was hiding, hoping the five brave souls making their way through the forest would rescue them from the malicious force that was on the verge of taking over.

Neeva slowed her pace, her eyes narrowing as she peered ahead into the darkness. "There," she whispered, pointing toward a clearing up ahead. "That's where I felt the magic strongest before. That clearing. It's where it all started."

She shook her head. "I wish I'd never gone in there."

Demetrius tensed, and for the first time, Holly realized he had a small blade in his hand.

"You think you're going to need that?"

"I have no idea, but I plan to be prepared. We don't know what we're walking into."

He was right about that. She tightened her grip on the bag of magical supplies. She had packed everything she could think of—crystals, herbs, protective charms—but she wasn't sure it would be enough. Whatever this thing was, it didn't seem to play by the rules of modern magic. Or by any rules, for that matter.

As they walked closer to the clearing, Holly's breath caught in her throat. The air here was acrid, but it felt different—thicker, darker, almost suffocating. It was like breathing smoke. The ground was bare, the snow melted away, leaving a ring of blackened earth in the center of the clearing. As if the forest itself had recoiled from whatever had happened here.

"This is where I tried to bind it," Neeva said, her voice barely a whisper. "But it fought back. The magic was too strong for me."

Flavia cocked one brow. "I can see that."

"Stinks of soot and sulfur," Charisma said.

Demetrius scanned the perimeter, his posture tense, ready for a fight. The blade remained in his hand. "Neeva, what's your best guess about what you released?"

Neeva swallowed hard. The lantern wobbled as she set it down at the edge of the clearing. "I don't know. I thought it was just old magic—something tied to the land, something I could control. But now I don't think it's that simple. I think it's ... something alive."

Holly's stomach twisted at the word. *Alive.* The dark magic wasn't just an energy or a force—it had a will of its own. It wanted something. And from what she'd seen, it wasn't going to stop until it got it.

Demetrius stepped forward, his eyes focused on the blackened earth at the center of the clearing. "Whatever it is, we have to stop it here. If it breaks free again, there's a good chance it'll be even stronger."

Holly took a deep breath, steeling herself as she stepped into the clearing beside Demetrius. She would have given anything to be back in the cabin, a Christmas movie on the television, a bowl of popcorn nearby, and her knitting in her hands, but they had no choice. If they didn't stop the magic now, it might very well be the end of everything she loved.

"Neeva." Flavia tipped her head. "You're the one who released it. You need to help us bind it again."

"Tell us what to do," Charisma said.

Neeva nodded, though her face was pale with fear. "I'll try. But we'll need to work together. You can't leave me alone to do this. Whatever this magic is, it won't go down without a fight."

"You're not going to be alone," Holly said. "No matter what happens, we're going to be right here beside you."

Demetrius's expression held sheer determination as he looked around at the women. He twirled the dagger through his fingers. "If it wants a fight, then we'll give it a fight. Together."

Holly nodded as she reached into her bag and pulled out a handful of crystals and a pouch of salt and iron dust combined. Magic vibrated through the air, pulsing with a dark, hungry energy. The shadows at the edge of the clearing seemed to shift and move, like they were watching, waiting. Predatory.

It was a terrifying feeling to think of yourself as prey.

"Let's set up the circle," Holly said to her sister witches. "Demetrius, you'll need to keep watch. If the magic tries to break free, we'll need you to hold it off long enough for us to complete the binding."

Demetrius's gaze was hard and focused, his grip tight around the blade he still held. "I've got your backs. Do what you need to do."

Holly and the other women knelt down, their hands moving swiftly as they arranged the crystals and other materials they'd brought in a protective circle around the clearing.

Holly whispered words of power under her breath, feeling the magic rise inside her, warm and familiar, as it spread through the circle. Neeva worked a few feet away from Holly, her hands moving with practiced precision as she added the protective herbs and whispered her own incantations, just as Charisma and Flavia were doing.

The air crackled with energy, the dark magic swirling just beyond the edge of the circle, like a hunter stalking its target. It seemed almost like it knew what they were getting ready to do. Maybe it did.

Not a thought Holly took comfort in.

"Hurry," Demetrius growled, his eyes locked on the shadows that seemed to be creeping closer.

"I'm done," Charisma said, standing up.

"So am I," Flavia added.

"Same," Holly chimed in as she got to her feet, too.

A second later, Neeva lifted her hands. "Finished."

"Then let's cast this spell and go home," Holly said.

The women raised their hands, stretching them toward one another, and began to speak the words that would contain the dark magic.

The tension in the air doubled, the magic straining against the protective circle they had created. Now, within the circle, a slow-moving whirlwind of gray, sooty tendrils spun out of the ground in the center of it. The whirlwind grew, expanding, darkening, reaching the limits of the circle, where the four women stood just outside of it.

A low rumble bellowed out of it, then a few flashes of angry lightning shot through the miasma of twisting shadows.

The darkness took on an angry purple glimmer almost as if Holly and her sister witches were bruising it. The dark force definitely knew they were trying to bind it, and it was testing the protection spell they'd just cast to see how strong it was.

Suddenly, a low, guttural hiss filled the air, and Holly's heart lurched with the realization that the whirlwind *hadn't* been just a test. It had also been a signal calling out to the other strands of itself that had already managed to slither free from the earth. The shadows at the edge of the clearing surged forward, twisting and writhing like living creatures.

Inside the circle, the furious dark magic had come to life. There was a face inside it. The face of Morgana.

A chill sluiced through Holly. No wonder the woman had disappeared.

Morgana snarled at them, her shadow face huge and looming. "You will not win this time, little witch."

"Yes, I will, Morgana! You have no idea what you're up against!" Except she did. She knew exactly what Holly was capable of, thanks to their first encounter.

"We got your back," Flavia yelled. "We won't let her touch you, Holly."

"Thanks!" But then Holly shouted for Demetrius, her voice tight with panic as she feared for his safety. "Demetrius, look out!"

Morgana was contained within the circle, but the shadows coming out of the forest were coming for him.

"I see them." Demetrius didn't hesitate. He lunged forward, his body a blur of motion as he placed himself between Holly and the oncoming darkness. The blade flashed in his hands, his eyes glowed a brilliant silver, and his fangs were bared as he faced off against the menacing figures.

The dark magic hissed and snarled, but Demetrius held his ground, his presence as steady and unyielding as a wall. He moved with the speed and precision of an apex predator, his blade glinting in the dim light as he sliced through the shadows, keeping them at bay.

Holly knew that wasn't just any blade. It had magic in it to wield such power against that kind of darkness.

"We're running out of time," Neeva said as she worked beside Holly, her hands shaking with the strain of holding the circle together. "The magic is too strong—we can't contain it."

"Morgana is gaining on us," Flavia yelled.

"Don't think that way! We can do this!" Holly's mind raced, desperation clawing at her as she struggled to keep the circle intact. The magic was growing stronger, more violent, and she could feel it slipping through her fingers. They weren't going to make it.

"This is old magic," Charisma shouted. "Only old magic can fight old magic. I'm not sure—" Her words ended in a grunt as she dodged a purple tendril that had swiped at her.

Old magic. In a flash of clarity, Holly remembered something—something her grandmother had told her more than once about the Winters family magic. It wasn't just about protection. It was about *balance.*

"Neeva, Flavia, Charisma," Holly said, the urgency in her voice making it carry above the chaos. "We're not going to bind it. We're going to balance it."

Morgana howled in fury, but the women ignored her. The three witches gave Holly their attention, but it was Neeva who spoke, wide-eyed and blinking. "What? How?"

"The magic is tied to the land," Holly said as the pieces fell into place. "Morgana feels like proof of that. So it's part of the natural order. If we try to bind it, it'll keep fighting back. But if we balance it—if we restore the balance between light and dark—it'll settle. It'll go back to where it belongs. Taking Morgana with it."

Flavia shook her head. "How do you know that?"

Holly shrugged. "Old family magic? I just do. Trust me. Please. I can feel this is the right way."

"We trust you," Charisma said.

Neeva stared at her for a moment, then nodded, her face set with determination. "She's right. We do. Let's get this done."

"Okay," Holly said. "Follow me."

Morgana raged against the boundaries of the circle as Holly began to knit a new spell—a spell not of binding but of balance. Charisma, Flavia, and Neeva followed her lead, calling on the ancient magic of the land, the same magic that had flowed through Nocturne Falls for years. The magic that had called the Ellinghams here. The magic Alice had channeled into when she'd cast her own protective magic all those years ago.

Under Demetrius's watchful gaze, the four women guided threads of light and dark, weaving a tapestry that contained both life and death, bringing equal parts of nature and magic into harmony.

The air around them teemed with energy, tiny sparks of it floating through the air like embers caught on the wind. Holly could feel the magic responding, shifting, as if the forest itself was waking up. The shadows stopped writhing, their violent movements slowing as the balance began to take hold.

With a final, guttural cry, Morgana faded into mist.

"It's working," Demetrius whispered. He stepped back, his eyes fixed on the dark magic as it swirled in place, no longer attacking but simply ... existing.

"We're doing it," Neeva breathed, her voice filled with awe.

Charisma and Flavia nodded, smiles of utter amazement on their faces, hands lifted as they continued to balance the forces before them.

Holly could feel it too—the magic settling and calming as the balance was restored. The darkness wasn't gone, but it was no longer a threat. It was part of the natural order, part of the land.

As the final segment of the spell took hold, the shadows faded, the tendrils sank back into the earth, and the air around them grew still. The clearing was quiet and the dark magic dormant again. Not by force but by balance.

Holly collapsed to the ground, her body trembling with exhaustion. She couldn't remember ever feeling this drained, but never had she been so relieved. So happy. She exhaled, then breathed in a lungful of crisp winter air.

Demetrius knelt beside her, his hand resting gently on her shoulder. "You okay?"

She nodded. "Yeah, just wiped out."

"You did it. Morgana and the darkness are gone."

Holly looked at him, then the three other women, a tired smile tugging at her lips. "*We* did it."

Neeva stood at the edge of the clearing, her face pale but her eyes filled with wonder. "It's over. The magic ... it's part of the land again. This will never be a problem again. I hope."

Holly nodded, her heart swelling with a mixture of relief and pride. They had done it. They had stopped the dark magic—not by fighting it but by understanding it. By restoring the balance. Just like her grandmother had told her.

Demetrius gave Holly a hand up. "Come on. Let's go home."

As the five of them made their way back through the forest, snow started to fall softly around them. Holly stuck her hand out, catching one perfect flake on her glove. A deep sense of peace settled over her. The darkness had been part of Nocturne Falls all along, and now, thanks to her grandmother's wisdom, it was no longer a threat to the town or anyone in it.

With Demetrius guarding them, she and her sister witches had faced the darkness—and won.

But more importantly, they had faced it together.

14

The next morning, Holly woke to the soft glow of sunlight streaming through the cabin's frosted windows. The warmth of the light was a welcome contrast to the cold, dark magic they'd fought in the forest the night before. For the first time in days, the tension in her body began to ease, replaced by a quiet sense of calm.

She stretched, feeling the stiffness in her muscles from the exertion of the spell. Her whole body was a little achy, and her mind felt like it had run a marathon, but there was relief in knowing they had stopped the threat.

Hexi was nowhere in sight. That had to mean he'd already gone looking for breakfast. She pulled on her robe and went out to the living room.

Demetrius, who'd insisted on standing guard just in case, was already up, if he'd even slept. He stood in his usual spot by the front windows, his back to her. He was silhouetted against the morning light, and Holly couldn't help but admire the quiet strength he exuded, even when things had been at their worst. He had been a steady presence through it all, protecting her, standing by her side without hesitation.

"Morning," she said, her voice still rough with sleep. "Still all clear out there?"

Demetrius glanced over his shoulder, his expression softening just slightly when he saw her. "Still all clear. No sign of Morgana or anything you need to be worried about. How are you feeling?"

"Tired," Holly admitted, rubbing her eyes. "But I think I'll survive."

Demetrius nodded, his eyes thoughtful as he turned back to the window. "You did an amazing job last night."

"Thanks." Holly smiled faintly, remembering how willing he'd been to defend them against the dark magic. "We all did. I can't believe Morgana was part of it. I knew there was something off about her."

"I felt it too. Something about her was definitely not right. Oh, by the way, I fed the cats. It was that or I thought Hexi might bite me."

She laughed. "Sounds about right. Thanks." That explained Hexi's absence.

Demetrius's gaze stayed on the woods beyond the cabin, his expression unreadable. "The magic is still out there, you know. It's quieter now, but it's not gone. I don't mean Morgana. Just the presence of whatever created her."

Holly's stomach twisted at the reminder. They had restored the balance, but the dark magic was still present. It always would be. It was in the land, woven into the very fabric of the town. They hadn't destroyed it—they had simply kept it from consuming everything in its path.

"I know," Holly said, her voice quiet. "But it feels

different now, don't you think? Calmer. Almost like it's been changed."

Demetrius offered her a small, almost imperceptible smile. "That's because you balanced it. You didn't fight the magic—you understood it. Very impressive."

"For a witch like me?"

"For anyone." The tiny smile morphed into a real one. "*You* are very impressive."

Holly's body warmed at his words, though she couldn't shake the lingering unease. She had always thought of magic as something that could be controlled, something she could bend to her will. But now she understood that some forces were bigger than any one person—bigger than any spell. And those forces had to be respected, not fought.

Quite a tough way to learn that lesson, but she certainly wouldn't forget it.

Just then, there was a soft knock at the door. Holly jumped.

Demetrius frowned. "I'll get it."

When Holly saw Neeva standing in the doorway, her hands clasped in front of her nervously, Holly let out a sigh of relief. "Hi."

Neeva stepped inside, her face still pale but her expression softer than it had been the night before. "Hi. I —I wanted to thank you both. For helping me fix what I'd done."

Holly stood, brushing the sleep from her eyes as she

approached Neeva. "We couldn't have done it without your help."

Neeva shook her head, guilt still shadowing her features. "I should never have messed with that magic. I thought I could control it, but I was wrong. I'm sorry for putting you both in danger. For putting us all in danger."

Demetrius crossed his arms, watching Neeva carefully, but his expression wasn't as disapproving as it had been. He was clearly all right with allowing her to make amends.

"It's done now," Holly said gently. "And thanks to your help, we fixed it and it's not a threat to us or the town anymore. That's what matters. Besides, it's the Christmas spirit to forgive."

Neeva nodded, though she still seemed unsure. "I wanted to make things right. I've caused enough damage in this town, and I don't want anyone else to get hurt."

"You did that." Holly smiled, the warmth of her magic thrumming just beneath her skin. "But you can certainly help us keep an eye on the magic. It's part of Nocturne Falls now, but that doesn't mean we can let our guard down."

Neeva's eyes brightened slightly, relief washing over her features. "I'd like that. I owe it to the town."

Demetrius nodded in agreement, his voice low but firm. "We all do."

The three of them stood in the quiet of the cabin, the sunlight streaming in through the windows, casting beams of light across the room. Holly's hope had returned—not just for herself but for the town. They had faced the darkness and come out the other side, and now they had a chance to move forward.

As Neeva excused herself, promising to return later to discuss the next steps, Holly turned to Demetrius, her heart full but still heavy with the weight of everything they had been through. It was going to take a little time to put that completely behind her.

"What happens now?" she asked quietly. Exhaustion was starting to catch up to her.

Demetrius's eyes met hers, and for a moment, she saw something in his gaze—something deeper, more vulnerable than she'd ever seen before. "Now we keep going. We keep watch, we protect the town, and we make sure the magic stays balanced."

Holly nodded, the weight of his words settling over her. But there was something else between them, something unspoken, that lingered in the air. She had grown closer to Demetrius over the past few days—closer than she ever imagined possible. He had been there for her in ways she hadn't expected, and now that the immediate danger had passed, she didn't want to lose that connection.

"Demetrius," she began, hesitant. "I couldn't have done this without you. I mean that. Thank you."

Demetrius gave her a small smile, his eyes softening as he looked at her. "You're welcome. I've said it before, but it bears repeating. You're stronger than you think, Holly. Still, I'm glad I was here."

Warmth spread through her, and she allowed herself to acknowledge the feelings that had been simmering just beneath the surface. Demetrius wasn't just her protector or her ally—he had become something more. And as much as she had tried to deny it, she couldn't ignore it any longer. She had feelings for him, feelings she'd never wanted, but there was no turning away from them now.

"I'm glad you were here too," she said, her voice barely above a whisper.

For a moment, a deep silence spread between them, the air thick with unspoken words. Demetrius's gaze lingered on hers, and Holly's heart raced as she wondered what he was thinking—what he was feeling.

He reached for her, but before either of them could say or do anything, there was another knock at the door.

Holly blinked, the moment shattered as she turned toward the sound. She opened the door to find Flavia standing on the porch, her cheeks flushed from the cold, a bright smile on her face. She held a white cardboard box in her hands, the warm aroma of cinnamon wafting from it.

"Sorry, I just had to come by and check on you," Flavia said, stepping inside and shaking the snow from her coat. She held the box out. "And bring you this. A cinnamon bun from Mummy's, fresh from the oven. Thought you might need a little something. How are you doing? Are you all right?"

Holly smiled, grateful for the distraction, even though

her heart still fluttered from the moment she'd almost shared with Demetrius. She took the box. "Thank you for the cinnamon bun. It smells great. I'm fine. Still a bit tired, but I suppose that's to be expected. Thanks for your help, too. You and Charisma were fantastic. I couldn't have done that without you. I owe you both."

"You owe us nothing. We were happy to help." Flavia's eyes twinkled with curiosity as she glanced at Demetrius. "You know, the town's been buzzing about what happened. No one knows the full story, but word's spread, and there's talk about some kind of ancient magic being released and Morgana's part in it."

Holly exchanged a glance with Demetrius, her smile fading slightly. "Yeah, well, let's just say Nocturne Falls has a little more magic in it now than we realized."

Flavia's smile brightened. "I'm just glad you're safe. That we're all safe. And if there's anything the coven can do to help, just say the word."

Holly nodded, her heart warming at the offer. "Thanks, Flavia. I'll let you know. We probably just need to make the coven aware of everything that happened and to let them know to keep an eye out for any strange occurrences. That would be helpful."

"Stranger than usual, you mean?"

Holly laughed. "Exactly."

As Flavia chatted for a few more minutes, catching Holly up on the latest gossip in town, Holly felt a sense of normalcy returning. The danger had passed, and life in Nocturne Falls was back to its usual quirky self. But as

Flavia left, Holly couldn't ignore the way her heart tugged toward Demetrius.

When the door closed behind Flavia, Holly turned to find Demetrius watching her, his expression unreadable once again.

"Everything okay?" he asked, his voice low.

Holly nodded, though her heart still raced. "Yeah. I just ... I've been thinking."

Demetrius raised an eyebrow, waiting.

Holly took a deep breath and started toward the kitchen. "You want some of this cinnamon bun? They're fantastic."

He followed, as she'd expected. "You were thinking about whether or not I'd want some cinnamon bun?"

She smiled. "No." She opened the box. The pastry was enormous and smelled like everything that was right in the world. She got out a knife and two plates. "I was thinking, I don't know what's going to happen next. With the magic, with Nocturne Falls ... with us." Just saying the word made her nervous, because what if she was over-thinking this and there wasn't an us? What if this attraction was all one-sided? Her side alone. She took a breath. "I do know that I want you here. I want you to stay. In my life."

Demetrius's pupils widened, and for a moment, Holly thought she saw a flicker of emotion—something raw and real—flash across his face. He stepped closer, his voice a low murmur. "I'm not going anywhere, Holly. I've decided I need to stay in Nocturne Falls. Any doubts I had are gone. This is where I want to be. In fact, I want to put down roots for once in my life."

Holly's heart swelled at his words, and she let out a breath she hadn't realized she'd been holding. "I love that idea."

Demetrius's mouth curved into a small, almost shy smile, and Holly couldn't help but smile back. They had faced the darkness together, and they had come out the other side stronger, closer. Whatever happened next would probably be an even bigger adventure.

He bent closer and kissed her. She shut her eyes and sank into him, easing her hands onto his chest as his cupped her elbows. The kiss was sweet and soft and tentative, both of them figuring out this new ground together.

She'd never again smell cinnamon without thinking of him.

They broke apart, each smiling, each quiet with the wonder of what had just happened.

As the light of the winter morning filled the cabin, Holly felt a sense of peace settle over her. The dark magic might still be out there, lurking in the shadows, but for now, there was light. There was warmth. And there was hope.

And that was enough.

For now.

The late afternoon sun cast a golden blush over the snow-covered landscape, turning the forest into a shimmering sea of white and peach. Holly sat by the fire, absently running her fingers through Hexi's soft fur as she stared into the crackling flames. Demetrius was on the couch with Moonshadow and his book. *Miracle on 34th Street* played on the television, but the sound was down low, and neither of them was really watching it.

Otherwise, the cabin was quiet, the tension from the past few days finally beginning to ebb away. But even in the stillness, her mind wouldn't stop.

Neeva had spent the day helping Holly reinforce the protection spells around the cabin, carefully layering the magic they would need to ensure the dark forces remained at bay. The two witches had worked in silence for the most part, the weight of everything that had occurred still heavy on their shoulders.

Neeva had even helped Holly recast the barrier. But now, as the day drew to a close, Holly sensed that Neeva was going to move on. Call it intuition or a witch's sixth sense, but that's what Holly had begun to anticipate.

Neeva had helped repair the damage she had caused, but Holly had the feeling the woman no longer wanted to be where the reminder of her mistake was so present. Holly wasn't sure where Neeva would go, but she perceived the older witch, who was still apologizing for what had happened, needed space to heal from her own mistakes.

At the moment, she was in Holly's bathroom, freshening up before she went home.

Neeva came out and stood near the door, her coat draped over her arm, her expression thoughtful. She had been quiet all afternoon, but Holly could see the change in her—the guilt and fear that had once clouded her eyes had finally given way to something else. Something lighter.

"Thank you for being so understanding about everything, but it's time for me to go," Neeva said softly, breaking the silence. Her voice, though hesitant, held a note of resolution. "Not just home, but ... somewhere else. I've done what I can here."

Holly stood, brushing a stray lock of hair behind her ear, not surprised her premonition had come true. "You've done a lot. We wouldn't have been able to stop the magic without you. That's not even a question."

Neeva gave a small, wistful smile, her hands wringing the edges of her coat. "I just wish I hadn't been the one to set it free in the first place."

"We all make mistakes," Holly said gently, crossing the room to stand beside her. "What matters is that you stayed and helped fix it. You faced it. Please promise me you'll forgive yourself? We all have."

Demetrius nodded. "She's right. No one has any hard feelings toward you. It could have happened to anyone."

"Thanks," Neeva said, her eyes shining with unshed tears. "I will try. I don't know what's next for me, but ... I need to figure it out. Maybe a fresh start somewhere else would be just the thing."

Holly reached out, placing her hand on Neeva's arm. "You're welcome in Nocturne Falls anytime. I mean that. You don't have to leave for good."

Neeva hesitated, then nodded, though her smile remained distant. "Thank you both. I'll remember that."

With a final glance at Demetrius, who now had Moonshadow on his lap, Neeva pulled her coat on and reached for the door handle. Holly walked her out, the cold air nipping at her face as they stepped onto the porch.

The snow had stopped falling, and the world around them was quiet, as if holding its breath. Neeva turned to Holly, her eyes full of gratitude and something that looked very much like hope.

"Take care of yourself," Holly said, offering a warm smile. "And if you ever need help, you know where to find me. Us," she quickly added.

Neeva gave her a little smile. "That's kind of you. Thanks, Holly. For everything. And Merry Christmas."

"Merry Christmas, Neeva."

And with that, Neeva turned and walked down the steps toward her car. Holly watched her, the stillness of the evening settling over the world like a blanket. She took a deep breath, feeling a sense of closure, as Neeva got into her car and drove off, disappearing down the road.

When Holly finally turned back toward the cabin, she found Demetrius standing in the doorway, his hands in his pockets, his gaze fixed on her. The enormity of everything they had been through hung in the air between them, but for the first time in days, they had space to breathe. Like the storm had passed and now they could move forward under blue skies.

"Neeva's gone," Holly said, stepping back inside and closing the door behind her. The warmth of the fire wrapped around her like an embrace, and she couldn't help but feel a strange sense of relief. Not just because the darkness had receded and things had been put right again but because Demetrius was still there.

She couldn't deny his presence gave her a sense of peace and protection she'd never felt alone.

Demetrius nodded, his gray eyes soft as he watched her. "She needed to leave, and she knew that. She has her own path to follow. I give her a lot of respect for being brave enough to understand that and act on it."

Holly nodded, moving to sit in her armchair by the fire again. Hexi had already curled back up on the hearthrug, purring contentedly, while Moonshadow stretched luxuriously on the couch, seemingly unbothered by the events of the past few days.

Such was a cat's life.

For a long moment, neither Holly nor Demetrius

spoke, the crackle of the fire and the movie dialogue the only sounds in the room. The emotional whirlwind of the past few days had worn her out, but sitting here with Demetrius, she felt safe and newly energized.

More than that. She felt something she hadn't thought possible. She felt loved by someone outside her family. Which wasn't to say she thought Demetrius was on the point of proposing. She just knew he cared, and that meant a lot.

"I'm glad it's over," Holly said quietly, her eyes fixed on the flickering flames. "But I can't help thinking ... what now?"

Demetrius took the other armchair, sitting on the edge of the seat as if he wanted to be as close to her as possible, his gaze thoughtful. "Whatever comes next, we'll handle it."

Holly imagined there was a vulnerability in her eyes she couldn't hide, but she didn't care. She wanted him to know how she felt. "I don't know what I would've done without you, Demetrius. You've been ... more than I could have asked for."

Demetrius glanced at his hands. "You didn't need me —you handled the magic on your own. You were a force to be reckoned with."

Holly shook her head, her pulse ticking up as he lifted his head, and she met his gaze. "Maybe I could've handled the magic. But it wasn't just the magic. You were there for me, Demetrius. You've kept me grounded. You've been ... my anchor. My support. My protector.

And I got the sense that you weren't just doing it out of duty."

For a moment, there was silence. Demetrius's eyes searched hers, and Holly felt her body go warm under the intensity of his gaze. She had never allowed herself to think too deeply about the connection between them, but now, in the quiet of the cabin, with the storm behind them, she couldn't ignore it anymore.

"I didn't expect any of this," Holly whispered, her voice trembling slightly. "Not the storm, not the magic, certainly not ... you."

Demetrius's eyes filled with a look that made Holly's heart skip a beat. He leaned in just a little, his voice a low murmur. "I didn't expect any of this either. But I like it. I like you. A *lot*."

Holly's breath caught in her throat as she looked at him, her heart thumping so loudly, she knew he had to hear it. There was something that had been simmering beneath the surface since the moment they had met. And now, with nothing standing in their way, it was impossible to ignore.

"Demetrius ..." Holly began, but her words trailed off as Demetrius reached out, his hand gently brushing against hers. His touch was cool but steady, and Holly felt a rush of warmth spread through her at the contact.

"I'm not going anywhere, Holly," Demetrius said softly, his eyes never leaving hers. "I've told you that, and I'll make it a promise now. I will be here until you don't want me to be."

She couldn't imagine that happening. Her heart swelled at his words, and for the first time in a long time, she allowed herself to feel what she had been trying to deny. She had grown to care about Demetrius more than she had ever expected. And now, she didn't want to lose him.

"I don't want you to go," Holly whispered, her voice barely audible. "I can't imagine wanting that."

Demetrius's mouth curved into a small smile, and in that moment, Holly saw something she hadn't seen in him before—vulnerability. He wasn't just the stoic, brooding vampire who had been her protector. He was someone who had come to mean more to her than she had ever thought possible.

Without thinking, Holly leaned forward, closing the distance between them. Her heart raced as she initiated the kiss this time, pressing her lips to his, the warmth of the fire and the softness of the moment wrapping around them like a cocoon.

Demetrius's hand came up to caress her cheek, his touch gentle, and emotion flooded through her. The weight of the darkness lifted, replaced by something lighter, something promising. Something that felt like the future.

When they finally pulled apart, Holly's breath was shaky, but her heart was full. Demetrius held on to her hand, and she knew that the walls he had built around himself had begun to crumble.

"You should probably know I won't be easy to get rid

of. I will fight to keep you, I promise you that," Demetrius said, his voice a low murmur. "But have patience with me. This whole relationship thing is not something I'm great at. Hard to admit that, but it's true."

Holly smiled, her heart swelling with affection. "I think honesty is a great way to start being great at it. It's kind of new for me, too. So we'll be patient with each other, okay?"

"I like that."

As they sat together by the fire, the cabin warm and filled with a quiet sense of peace, Holly knew that whatever came next—whether it was dark magic, supernatural chaos, or just the everyday challenges of life—they would figure it out together.

It was crazy, but Holly felt like she had finally found where she was meant to be. Not just in Nocturne Falls but with Demetrius. What an amazing Christmas Eve this was.

They had faced the darkness, and now they had the chance to build something new.

Together. Which was probably the best Christmas gift she'd had in a long time.

16

The soft glow of the twinkling lights on the little tree filled the cabin as Christmas morning dawned over Nocturne Falls. Snow blanketed the world outside, turning the forest into a glittering wonderland.

Inside, the warmth of the fire crackled in the hearth, casting a cozy glow across the room, and the scent of cinnamon and pine filled the air. Holly sat at the kitchen table.

Demetrius, settling into domestic life in a way he'd never thought possible, was making coffee. His dormant heart felt surprisingly light for the first time in what might have been forever. Was this love? He wasn't sure, but it certainly seemed like it.

He'd even stopped thinking about Esme, except for the occasional reminder of how very different Holly was.

Hexi was curled up on her lap, purring contentedly, while Moonie lounged on the couch in the living room. The peace in the cabin felt like a long-lost gift, a contrast to the tension and danger they had faced just days before.

He knew he'd have to go back to his place eventually. The road was plowed. He was out of excuses. He just didn't want to leave Holly. Not that they were so far away from each other, but at the moment, they were living in this perfect little bubble of time and space. He didn't want to break it, even though he knew it was inevitable.

He pressed the button to start the coffee brewing. He turned to look at Holly. "This is nice, isn't it?"

"It's very nice," she said. She'd been quieter than usual that morning, but he knew her well enough by now to know that she was simply enjoying the calm—letting herself relax after everything they had been through. "I like having someone make coffee for me."

He laughed softly. He'd gladly do it for her every morning. When the coffee was done, he poured them each a cup. Maybe Christmas morning coffee could be a new tradition for them. The idea gave him a curious and unexpected sense of joy.

Who was he? Who was this person smiling and bantering with the beautiful, quirky woman that had inexplicably stolen his heart? He didn't know, but he liked this version of himself. That in itself was something new and amazing.

She sipped her coffee, watching Demetrius from under her lashes, but he knew he was being scrutinized. Well, she could look all she wanted to.

"Enjoying the view?" he finally asked playfully.

Holly gave a quick nod. "Yeah, I am. Merry Christmas, by the way."

Her quick change of subject did nothing to stop the color rising in her cheeks. It was sweet and innocent in a way that made it impossible for him not to smile. She was something else, this knitting, cat-loving, gorgeous, kind, sweeter than sweet witch.

After everything they had been through, it felt strange —wonderful, even—to be here, in the quiet of Christmas morning, with Holly by his side. He hadn't expected to find happiness again, not after the life he'd lived. But here he was, and it was all because of her.

"You want to go watch a cheesy Christmas movie and eat the rest of that cinnamon bun?"

He nodded. "That sounds perfect."

Holly warmed up the remaining half of the cinnamon bun, then cut it and put it on two plates, which she carried out and set on the coffee table. He followed her to the living room, their coffee cups in hand.

"Come sit," Holly said, patting the cushion beside her on the couch. "It's Christmas, after all. You're supposed to do nothing."

Demetrius raised an eyebrow, even though he was grinning as he sat. "I'm not exactly the do-nothing type."

Holly laughed softly, shaking her head. "You've earned some downtime, Demetrius. We both have."

"That's for sure." With a low chuckle, Demetrius put his arm around her and kissed the side of her head.

While Holly flipped through the movie options, they sat in comfortable silence, the warmth of the fire and the contented purring of the cats filling the room.

Demetrius felt an upswell with something deeper than gratitude—something he couldn't remember feeling in a very long time.

This was home now. Nocturne Falls, this cabin, and Holly. His sprawling family estate would never feel like this, unless she was in it. Maybe she'd spend some time with him there. She could certainly bring Hexi. There was more than enough room.

All this time, he'd been expecting to spend Christmas alone, but instead, he had found something far more precious than he had ever imagined. Something he hadn't been looking for because he hadn't thought it was out there. Not for him, anyway.

"What are you thinking about?" Holly asked quietly, her voice cutting through his thoughts.

Demetrius smiled softly, glancing down at Moonie, who had nestled against his leg. "Just how different this Christmas is compared to last year. I never thought I could feel like this."

"And how is that?"

"Happy," he said, the word as sweet on his tongue as the cinnamon bun.

Holly's expression softened, her eyes studying him intently. "You deserve happiness, Demetrius."

The tenderness in her voice touched him. "So do you."

For a moment, they simply looked at each other, the weight of their shared experiences and unspoken emotions hanging in the air. Holly's breath hitched as Demetrius's hand brushed against hers, craving the feel of her warm, velvety skin.

Holly leaned forward, and without another thought, Demetrius closed the distance between them, his lips brushing against hers with the tenderness he felt toward her. Once upon a time, his greatest desire had been to be left alone.

Now all he wanted was to be with her. To protect her, to make her laugh, to make her as happy as she made him.

The kiss was soft, almost hesitant at first, but then it deepened, and he felt her melt into him. Demetrius's hand cupped her cheek to pull her closer. The warmth of the fire, the soft purring of the cats, and the muted sounds of the television all faded away, leaving only the two of them.

When they finally pulled apart, Holly's breath was ragged, and he could hear her pleasure in her pulse. She looked into his eyes, and he saw his own emotions reflected back at him.

"I didn't expect any of this," Demetrius murmured, his voice barely above a whisper, his forehead resting gently against hers. "But now that I have it ... now that I have you, I don't want to let it go."

Holly's fingers traced the line of his jaw. "You won't lose me, Demetrius. I'm not going anywhere."

For a long moment, they stayed like that, holding each other in the soft glow of the firelight, the warmth of the Christmas morning wrapping around them like a protective blanket. Demetrius felt a peace he hadn't known in years, and for the first time in a long time, he allowed himself to fully embrace it, because this time, he trusted that it was real.

This was what he had been searching for, what he hadn't even known he needed. Not just safety or protection—but a place to belong. And now he had found it. In Nocturne Falls. With Holly.

Hexi climbed into her lap and stretched so that his paws were on Demetrius's leg, his purring growing louder as if he approved of the new closeness between his humans. She chuckled. "I guess you've been accepted."

Moonie curled up tighter against him, like she was trying to get closer.

Demetrius glanced at the cats and nodded. "I think they're happy we've finally sorted ourselves out."

Holly laughed softly, resting her head on Demetrius's shoulder. "I'd have to agree with them."

She found them a movie, then he went into the kitchen to refill their coffees. They ate the leftover cinnamon bun, watching the movie and just enjoying the morning.

The world felt quiet, calm, and filled with possibility. He understood now that Christmas in Nocturne Falls wasn't just about holiday cheer—it was about magic, connection, and finding light in the darkest places.

They spent the rest of the day together, watching movies, playing board games, curled up by the fire, even going for a walk in the snow, which ended in a snowball fight that had them both laughing so hard they could barely speak.

As they warmed up by the fire, they enjoyed the peace they had fought so hard to protect. The cats moved between them, content and warm, the quiet sounds of their purring filling the room.

This, Demetrius thought, was happiness. At last. And if that wasn't a Christmas miracle, he wasn't sure what qualified.

As THE SKY darkened and evening fell, Holly realized something that made her heart flutter with joy.

This was the Christmas she had been waiting for. A Christmas filled with warmth, love, and hope. And with Demetrius by her side, she knew there would be many more to come.

"Demetrius," she said softly, glancing up at him as the fire crackled. He'd gotten up to add more wood to it.

"Hmm?" He looked back at her, his expression soft, the firelight giving him a warm glow.

"Merry Christmas," she whispered, her heart full.

Demetrius's eyes warmed, and he came back to press a gentle kiss to her forehead. "Merry Christmas, sweetheart."

In that moment, Holly knew that everything was exactly as it should be. The darkness was gone, and the light of Christmas filled her heart.

This was her new beginning. Her happily ever after. Her brooding vampire.

She smiled. Despite the near catastrophe, everything had worked out just right.

Want to be up to date on all books & release dates by Kristen Painter? Sign-up for my newsletter on my website, www.kristenpainter.com. No spam, just news (sales, freebies, and releases.)

If you loved the book and want to help the series grow, tell a friend about the book and take time to leave a review!

Other Books By Kristen Painter

PARANORMAL WOMEN'S FICTION

Midlife Fairy Tale Series:

The Accidental Queen

The Summer Palace

The Cloud Kingdom

First Fangs Club Series:

Sucks To Be Me

Suck It Up Buttercup

Sucker Punch

The Suck Stops Here

Embrace The Suck

Code Name: Mockingbird (A Paranormal Women's Fiction Novella)

COZY MYSTERY:

Jayne Frost Series:

Miss Frost Solves A Cold Case: A Nocturne Falls Mystery

Miss Frost Ices The Imp: A Nocturne Falls Mystery

Miss Frost Saves The Sandman: A Nocturne Falls Mystery

Miss Frost Cracks A Caper: A Nocturne Falls Mystery

When Birdie Babysat Spider: A Jayne Frost Short

Miss Frost Braves The Blizzard: A Nocturne Falls Mystery

Miss Frost Chills The Cheater: A Nocturne Falls Mystery

Miss Frost Says I Do: A Nocturne Falls Mystery

Lost in Las Vegas: A Frost And Crowe Mystery

Wrapped up in Christmas: A Frost And Crowe Mystery

Mystified In Music City: A Frost And Crowe Mystery

Nixed in New Orleans: A Frost And Crowe Mystery

Happily Everlasting Series:

Witchful Thinking

PARANORMAL ROMANCE

Nocturne Falls Series:

The Vampire's Mail Order Bride

The Werewolf Meets His Match

The Gargoyle Gets His Girl

The Professor Woos The Witch

The Witch's Halloween Hero – short story

The Werewolf's Christmas Wish – short story

The Vampire's Fake Fiancée

The Vampire's Valentine Surprise – short story

The Shifter Romances The Writer

The Vampire's True Love Trials – short story

The Dragon Finds Forever

The Vampire's Accidental Wife

The Reaper Rescues The Genie

The Detective Wins The Witch

The Vampire's Priceless Treasure

The Werewolf Dates The Deputy

The Siren Saves The Billionaire

The Vampire's Sunny Sweetheart

Death Dates The Oracle

The Vampire's Former Flame

Shadowvale Series:

The Trouble With Witches

The Vampire's Cursed Kiss

The Forgettable Miss French

Moody And The Beast

Her First Taste Of Fire

Monster In The Mirror

A Sky Full Of Stars

Sin City Collectors Series

Queen Of Hearts

Dead Man's Hand

Double or Nothing

Standalone Paranormal Romance:

Dark Kiss of the Reaper

Heart of Fire

Recipe for Magic

Miss Bramble and the Leviathan

All Fired Up

URBAN FANTASY

The House of Comarré series:

Forbidden Blood

Blood Rights

Flesh and Blood

Bad Blood

Out For Blood

Last Blood

The Crescent City series:

House of the Rising Sun

City of Eternal Night

Garden of Dreams and Desires

Nothing is completed without an amazing team.

Many thanks to:

Cover design: Janet Holmes using images under license from Shutterstock.com
Interior Formating: Gem Promotions
Editor: Chris Kridler

ABOUT THE AUTHOR

USA Today Best Selling Author Kristen Painter is a little obsessed with cats, books, chocolate, and shoes. It's a healthy mix. She loves to entertain her readers with interesting twists and unforgettable characters. She currently writes the best-selling paranormal romance series, Nocturne Falls, and award-winning urban fantasy. The former college English teacher can often be found all over social media where she loves to interact with readers.

For more information go to www.kristenpainter.com

Made in United States
North Haven, CT
13 March 2025

66775473R00095